Absence of Light

A CHARLIE FOX
THRILLER

Absence of Light

Zoë Sharp

FELONY & MAYHEM PRESS • NEW YORK

ABSENCE OF LIGHT

A Felony & Mayhem mystery

PRINTING HISTORY
First edition (Murderati Ink): 2013
Felony & Mayhem edition: 2016

Copyright © 2013 by Zoë Sharp
All rights reserved

ISBN: 978-1-63194-081-1

Manufactured in the United States of America

Printed on 100% recycled paper

Library of Congress Cataloging-in-Publication Data

Names: Sharp, Zoë, 1966- author.
Title: Absence of light : a Charlie Fox novella / Zoë Sharp.
Description: Felony & Mayhem edition. | New York : Felony & Mayhem Press,
2015. | ©2013 | Series: Charlie Fox | "A Felony & Mayhem mystery."
Identifiers: LCCN 2015046351 | ISBN 9781631940811 (softcover)
Subjects: LCSH: Fox, Charlie (Fictitious character)--Fiction. |
Bodyguards--Fiction. | GSAFD: Suspense fiction. | Mystery fiction.
Classification: LCC PR6119.H376 A63 2015 | DDC 823/.92--dc23
LC record available at http://lccn.loc.gov/2015046351

For the victims, survivors,
and rescue and recovery teams of the 2011
earthquake in Christchurch, New Zealand,
and of the 2010 earthquake in Haiti

The icon above says you're holding a copy of a book in the Felony & Mayhem "Hard Boiled" category. These books feature mean streets and meaner bad guys, with a cop or a PI usually carrying the story and landing a few punches besides. If you enjoy this book, you may well like other "Hard Boiled" titles from Felony & Mayhem Press.

———••◆••———

For more about these books, and other Felony & Mayhem titles, or to place an order, please visit our website at:

www.FelonyAndMayhem.com

Other "Hard Boiled" titles from

FELONY&MAYHEM

Absence of Light

One

THE LAST TIME I DIED they didn't get a chance to put me in the ground for it. Mind you, back then my apparent demise proved neither long nor durable. A brief but interminable period of nothingness between one stumbling heartbeat and a thousand-volt jumpstart.

It seemed the gods were determined to make up for that lapse by being unreasonably prompt this time.

The weird thing was that I remained fully conscious through it all, from the first violent buckling of the earth under my feet to this silent tomb.

Because it is silent now, and it shouldn't be.

The aftershock hit with very few of the warning signs I'd come to recognise. No initial trembling, no gradual increase in tremors as the seismic waves magnified from their distant, buried hypocentre. This one must have had its genesis almost directly beneath us, and not far down. The abrupt assault of released energy was more shocking than bullet or blade.

As I went down I didn't have time to offer more than a brief scream. One moment I was on the surface and the next the ground caved in around where I was standing. I smacked myself about quite a bit on the way to hell before I came to rest, lying trapped in utter darkness while the graunching shudders of the planet died away and I wondered if I'd be next to follow.

"Well, *shit*," I said aloud. My voice sounded muffled and very close.

The first small bubble of panic began to form under my ribcage. It brought with it a swell of nausea that prickled the hair on my scalp and sent a ripple of hot and cold rushing across the surface of my skin. I fought it all back, folded it up until I couldn't fold it any tighter, and packed it into a very small box hidden at the centre of me.

Lately that box had been getting overfull.

I ran through a quick mental checklist. Clearly I could still breathe although the solid weight pressing into my chest restricted how deeply. My left arm was wedged tight to my side. In fact, when I experimented I think it might have been pinned there by something that had pierced both forearm and abdomen and spiked the two together. I could feel an annoying trickle of blood under my shirt.

I could move my right arm and hand a little. Illogically, I wished I had a weapon in it, even though it would have done me no good. It wasn't that kind of fight.

My legs were numb. Best not to worry about what that might mean.

The normal rules of gravity did not seem to apply down there. With no real idea of my orientation I sucked up a ball of saliva and let it dribble from my lips. It ran diagonally outwards across my right cheek and ended, annoyingly, in my ear. Well, that answered the which-way-is-up question at least.

Carefully, I screwed my head round maybe half an inch or so to the left, scraping my forehead. My eyes strained for the faintest glimpse of daylight.

Nothing.

I might as well have been sealed into a sarcophagus.

I shut my eyes and diverted all sensory perception to my ears. I tried to tune out the ominous crunch of who knows how many tons of settling masonry and rubble above me and searched instead for anything that might conceivably have a human source.

It was then I caught the sound of sobbing.

"Hey!" I croaked, throat raw with dust. "Can you hear me?"

The sudden outward breath caused a flurry of grit to drop onto my tongue. I coughed and spat for a minute or so then worked my chin until I could nip the edge of my scarf with my teeth. I tugged the thin cotton up over my mouth as a filter before I tried again.

"Yes, yes, I'm here. Please!" came a distant voice. "Please, I'm bleeding. Help me!"

You and me both.

"Just keep calm," I called back. "They'll get us out."

The answer was laughter—harsh bordering on hysterical. I let them laugh-cry themselves back to speech without trying to hurry them through it. I wasn't exactly going anywhere. Christ, my left arm might have gone dead but the wound in my side felt as if it was starting to *boil*.

"They won't come for us," the voice managed eventually. "The *last* thing they'll do is get us out of here. Can't afford to. We know too much, you and I. We could tell too many stories. Stories they want to stay buried with us."

I didn't respond right away. Mainly because there was too much truth in the words to allow for an instant denial.

And also because the people who might be still up there, on the outside, were the very ones who had most to gain from the unfortunate accidental death of the pair of us.

"It's not just a job to them." I tried to push conviction into my tone and heard only a raw desperation. "It's a vocation. It's who they are. They will not abandon us."

They can't.

"Of course they will—in a heartbeat," my tomb partner insisted. "You think they have a choice?"

My suddenly arid mouth was a good excuse not to answer. In reality I was straining my ears, stretching out my senses as if they could be persuaded to catch the faintest sounds somewhere up there on the surface.

Sounds of a rescue team searching for us, digging for us, doing their best to keep us alive for long enough to bring us out to safety.

I heard nothing but silence.

And I saw nothing but the particular darkness that comes with a total absence of light.

Two

IT WAS ONLY a few days earlier that I got my first taste of what life was like in a major earthquake zone. People behaved differently, I found, as if to survive having their world quite literally turned upside down brought about a radical change in attitude.

The first sign was a certain ambivalence to the concept of danger. Perhaps that explained why the ex-Israeli Air Force pilot who nosedived us towards the half-destroyed runway laughed like a loon all the way down.

At the last moment he pulled back sharply to float the Lockheed C-130 Hercules into an approximate landing attitude and dumped the old heavy transport onto the ground from about six feet up, hard enough to make the airframe shudder. The pallets of netted-down cargo levitated briefly in the hold. I made sure to keep my feet well clear when they thumped down again.

The plane performed a couple of giant bounces that wouldn't have been out of place in a rodeo. Then the pilot yanked on the brakes as if hoping we'd all shoot forward to join him in the cockpit so we could congratulate him on his aviation prowess.

By the time we'd taxied off the flight-line my stomach was more or less back where nature intended. When I boarded the Hercules outside New York early that morning I hadn't expected comfort and amenities, which was fortunate. Our in-flight refreshment was a matter of helping yourself from the coffee urns strapped into the tail section.

Eventually we lurched to a stop and the four huge turboprops spooled down. After so many hours in the air, even wearing ear defenders, the relief was immense.

"There you go, guys," the pilot said, jumping down from the elevated cockpit and threading his way aft past the cargo as we unbuckled and stretched. "Perfect demonstration of the Khe Sanh Approach."

"Very impressive, Ari," I agreed. "Except we weren't trying to avoid groundfire on the way in."

He grinned. "Works just as good for short runways."

"At least he remembered to stop instead of just opening the ramp at the back and kicking us all out," said the guy next to me. "Had that happen a time or two."

He was a redheaded Scot called Wilson who came from one of the dodgier areas of Glasgow. An ex-Para now working for Strathclyde Police and currently on some kind of cultural exchange with the NYPD. He'd explained how a group of US officers had volunteered to help with the relief efforts and, for want of anything better, he'd stuck his hand up too.

Wilson had been fascinated by the idea of my work in close protection, envious of the pay and what he perceived as the glamour of travelling the world by private jet in the company of rock stars.

"Yeah," I told him, indicating the interior of the Herc. "Tell me about it."

He had a fund of war stories from his present and previous careers that had helped alleviate the boredom of a long flight with no creature comforts.

Even back in the military I'd never got used to the loo on a Hercules. It involved perching on a caravan-style construction built into high step at one side of the fuselage with a flimsy curtain pulled around you and very little to hold onto. Good job nobody had been attempting to use it during that final approach.

Transport aircraft pilots, in my experience, were different from jet jockeys in that they were mostly normal. Just my luck to end up with a lunatic who'd insisted on showing us how things were done during the Vietnam War. I was pretty sure Ari wasn't old enough to have seen action in that particular theatre, even if the venerable old aid-agency Herc he was flying might well have done.

We grabbed our kit bags and jogged down the lowered ramp which had already begun to swarm with ground crew off-loading supplies. I skipped sideways to avoid a forklift truck being driven with more gusto than expertise and stuck close to Wilson as we exited. At least he was a big enough target for them to avoid.

As I stepped down onto the concrete the warmth of the time and place finally hit me. I shrugged out of the jacket I'd worn for most of the flight. Like I said, a stripped-out transport plane doesn't even rival cattle-class on the most downmarket of budget airlines.

We headed towards what was left of the main terminal building. The control tower was still standing but the far end of the terminal itself had collapsed. It was my first glimpse of the damage a major earthquake leaves behind, this careless swatting of man's best construction efforts.

When I looked back I saw the reason for Ari the pilot's heroics with our landing. About two thirds of the way along, the runway had a diagonal line chopped across it as neatly as if someone had used a giant rotary saw. The concrete had split apart and heaved. One side of the small crevasse now stood a good two feet higher than the other.

"*That's* not going to be a cheap fix," I murmured.

Wilson slid me a quick smile. "Aye, an eight-point-six will do that to a city," he said. He hefted his bag onto his shoulder. "I assume you already know the roads between here and just about anywhere are out, by the way?" He nodded in the direction of a gleaming Eurocopter sporting the full-dress livery of the national police force. "That's my lift, by the looks of it, but I could probably get the local LEOs to drop you somewhere if you need it. Where you headed?"

The local Law Enforcement Officers he mentioned were standing around the helo all wearing combat-style uniforms along with equally uniform aviator sunglasses and moustaches. They had the look of men who would only be too delighted to drop me somewhere, providing it was a long way down.

"I'm fine, I think," I said. "I'm supposed to have a lift waiting but—"

"Coo-ee!"

The banshee cry was enough to make just about everyone in the vicinity turn and stare. A small bow-legged guy was ambling towards us. He had his hands in the pockets of his dusty combat pants and his booted feet scuffled the ground like he couldn't be bothered to lift them.

Above the combats he wore a multi-pocketed waistcoat of the kind favoured by fishermen and photographers, with no shirt underneath. Perhaps this was to show off the complexity of scars across his torso. From the tight irregularity of his skin I guessed he'd been badly burned at a time when the level of cosmetic surgery available had been a lot more rudimentary. So either he was proud of this visual history of his suffering or he simply didn't care.

I'd time to study his approach because he was completely focused on the guy standing next to me. I took in the newcomer's apparently relaxed face, deeply lined and tanned. It was completely at odds with the wariness I saw in his eyes.

"Charlie Fox, right?" he said to Wilson, sticking a hand out. "G'day, mate." His initial cry was suddenly explained by the strong if not slightly exaggerated Australian accent.

Wilson studied him for a beat, frowning, as if he'd seen the discrepancy between the face and eyes too and was working out what it might mean.

"Not me, pal," he said then, and jerked his head in my direction. "I think your lift has arrived." He took in the little Aussie's obvious consternation and gave me a slap on the shoulder. "See you round, Charlie. Our paths are bound to cross somewhere. And don't forget to mention me to your boss, next time he's recruiting, eh?"

"OK. Will do," I agreed, surprised he'd meant it serious enough to ask twice. "And good luck."

As Wilson strode away the Aussie said incredulously, "You're Charlie bloody Fox?"

"I've been called worse."

"But we asked for a security advisor, and you're…"

"Cheap, available, and here," I said cheerfully. "You're with Rescue & Recovery International, I take it?"

"R&R." His mouth corrected automatically while his brain was still playing catch-up. "Folks just call us R&R."

"And what do I call *you* that I can repeat in public?"

He shook his head although if he was hoping to shake some sense into it. I doubted it had much effect.

"Riley," he said then, and shook his head again.

I shifted my kit bag from one shoulder to the other. "Look, I've just had a very long, very uncomfortable trip with a pilot in desperate need of a nice white coat with sleeves that knot at the back," I said with tired calm. "I know damn well that your outfit's lead doctor is a woman and you've other female staff, so it's not like you've never seen anyone with lumps down the front of their shirt before. What's your problem with me?"

He finally gave me the same big friendly grin he'd broken out for Wilson, but this time with a sheepish tint to it.

"Jeez, sweetheart, it's nothing personal," he said, reaching for my bag. I swapped it to my furthest hand and kept a firm grip on the straps. "It's just that we've been having trouble with the locals. Supply chain's all to shit and natives have been getting a mite antsy. I was hoping for someone the size of your mate back there so I could hide behind 'em, y'know? I mean, you're practically as small as I am. Didn't eat your Wheaties as a kid, eh?"

"I know," I said, "but if it makes you feel better I move quick and I've got a very bad temper."

For a second he rocked back on his heels and regarded me, head on one side. "I'll bet," he said at last. "Y'know, Charlie, I get the feeling I'm gonna like you after all. C'mon then, the old bus is over by what's left of the hangar there, and light's a'wasting."

Three

RILEY'S "OLD BUS" turned out to be a Bell 212—
the civilian version of the twin-engined UH-1 Huey that's
been a staple of battlefields the world over since the late
sixties.

Not that this helicopter looked quite that old—or
particularly civilian. It had been painted some kind of matt-
finish sludge khaki colour with 'R&R' stencilled not quite
straight on the tail.

The passenger compartment, which could hold up to
fourteen seats, had been stripped down to the minimum
to leave room for cargo. It was currently half filled with a
cling-wrapped pallet of what looked to be medical supplies.
I wedged my kitbag alongside it and clipped a safety line
through the straps just to be sure.

I climbed into the co-pilot's seat, dragged on a set of
headphones held together with duct tape, and fastened my
belts. As I did so I noticed the butt of an old Ruger .357

Magnum sitting upside down in a canvas pocket slung alongside the pilot's seat.

"You expecting elephants?" I asked as Riley hauled himself in.

He grinned at me. "Wouldn't be the first time."

He let out a galumph of breath and rubbed both hands vigorously over his stubbled face. It reminded me of a long-distance truck driver who's already been on the road all night and still has too far to go.

Oh great. I survive being killed at the hands of a mad Israeli only to die at the hands of an equally mad Aussie.

"Been flying these things long?" I asked over the whine of the Pratt & Whitneys going through start-up.

"Got my licence about three months ago." Riley threw me a laconic smile as he juggled the controls and the Bell made an initial half-hearted attempt to get off the ground. "Well, to be fair, I should say I got it *back* three months ago. Here we go then!"

And with that he rammed the aircraft upward like an express elevator. We yawed drunkenly sideways as we rose, our downdraft flattening the wide grass runoff that bordered the service road. That was probably one of the reasons it was there.

Riley caught me gripping the bottom of my seat in reflex and didn't so much laugh as guffaw. The action that brought on a fit of coughing that made the Bell twitch in response to his hands.

"Relax, Charlie," he said when he could speak again. "It's like riding a bike. You don't really forget how to do it."

"Easy for you to say," I shot back. "Last time I was up in one of these damn things, we crashed."

"Hey, me too!" he said. "How about that?"

I was beginning to get the creeping sensation I was being taken for a ride in more ways than one but I didn't call him on it. I'd been through worse hazing, that was for sure. Better to let him have his fun and get it over with early.

Instead I adjusted the boom mic from my headset and asked, "So when did you R&R guys get in?"

"We set down inside about eight hours of the initial quake. Been working round the clock since then, more or less. She's a monster."

From the way he was slouched in his seat I realised he'd long ago adapted his wiry frame to the most comfortable position so he could keep to the schedule. Either that or all the scar tissue was twisting his body out of shape.

I looked out through the canopy and the Plexiglas panel by my feet, trying to ignore the jerkiness of the ride. Below me were swathes of destruction, buildings knocked flat as if a petulant child had gone rampaging across a beach full of sandcastles wearing bovver boots. From up there the whole scene lacked a sense of reality.

Most scary to me were the gaping holes that had opened up in the roads, fields and where the houses used to stand. I shivered. Having a building fall around your ears was one thing. Having the earth open up underneath your feet to sending you plummeting into the bowels was quite another.

The ground had contracted as well as split. I saw a wooden fence that had once been straight and was now an absurdly wiggled line, and a section of railway track that was distorted as a painting by Salvador Dalí.

"How bad are the casualties?"

Riley shrugged. "Over three hundred confirmed dead so far. We haven't really started digging out the bodies yet—still concentrating on finding survivors, y'know?" he said in a flat voice. "But if they don't get their supply lines sorted soon, that figure's going to rocket. There's already trouble about aid distribution, been some looting, stuff like that. Can get a bit hairy out there."

One of Wilson's tasks, so he'd told me on the flight, was likely to be ironing out those distribution kinks and maintaining order. I'd lay bets the big Scot would be good at it, even if he was going to have his work cut out.

"In that case I'm surprised you came in-country without a security advisor in place," I said as casually as I could manage.

Riley flicked me a quick look and gave another shrug. The action caused us to sideslip wildly to the left. "Never know how bad it's gonna be 'til you get here," he said, overcorrecting. "Besides, we lost our regular guy last time out."

"'Lost'?" I echoed. "'Lost' as in 'misplaced'? What happened?"

Before he could reply the cockpit radio squawked. Riley cut the intercom connection between us to answer it.

"Yeah doc, go ahead," I heard him say, only just audible to me over the roar of engine and rotor. "Not far. I'm giving Charlie the ten-dollar tour." There was a pause while the person on the other end clearly asked who the hell he was talking about. "Our new security expert," he said then, flashing his yellowed teeth. "Yeah, that's right. I tell you, I feel safer already."

I turned my head deliberately to stare out across the ruined cityscape. Columns of smoke still rose from the sporadic fires that had yet to be dampened. I could see groups of people scattered about the debris. Most wore fluorescent jackets or bibs. I knew it was a co-ordinated effort but their movements seemed small and futile against the sheer scale of the disaster.

There was a click in my ears and Riley's voice was back. "Gotta make a small diversion," he said.

"As long as the meter's not still running."

He laughed again. I waited in alarm for one of his lungs to make an actual appearance but he managed to choke it back down. "No worries," he said. "This one's on doctor's orders. Wants me to pick something up for her on the way in."

He swooped the Bell into a sudden stomach-dropping right-hand turn that tipped my side of the cockpit over by almost ninety degrees. It was like being back in the Hercules all over again.

I made another grab for my seat and realised, as the Aussie's wheezy laughter echoed in my ears, that he had just very neatly sidestepped answering my last question. The one about what had happened to my predecessor.

Perhaps, if I survived this flight, I'd get to ask him again.

Four

"**W**HEN YOU SAID you were going to 'pick something up' on the way, I thought you were talking about a pint of milk," I said.

"Jeez, don't put that idea in the doc's head for Christ's sake or she'll have us running all over this bloody city looking for unsweetened organic soy or some shit like that."

Riley put the Bell into a clumsy hover above a cracked roadway that curved dangerously close to the edge of a steep drop-off. He held it there for a moment or so while he checked around him and then didn't so much land as dump it onto the skids. We hit hard enough to loosen a few fillings—and the teeth that contained them.

If this was all part of his act to scare the newbie, I decided, it was getting very old very fast.

Still, better that than the alternative explanation—that he really *was* a dreadful pilot.

The Aussie climbed out and staggered for a few strides until his joints began functioning normally, leaving the Bell's engines on tick-over and the rotors turning lazily overhead. He was small enough that he didn't bother to duck.

I hopped out to join him without waiting for an invitation that clearly wasn't about to be issued. I assumed he left the helo in Park with the handbrake applied.

By the time I caught up, Riley was standing a foot or so back from the precipice next to another man. The newcomer was maybe a few years younger, his hair dark but flecked with grey. He wore coveralls with a rappelling harness and fluorescent bib over the top, and carried heavy gloves. There was a large coil of climbing rope at his feet.

Even without the high-and-tight buzzcut and the unbending stance, I would have pegged him as ex-military. There's an air about former US Marines they never seem to lose.

Both men were peering downwards. I moved alongside and did the same.

It immediately became clear why the narrow road appeared to run so close to the edge. Before the quake, it had been a dual carriageway positioned what should have been a safe distance back.

Now the entire left-hand lane and shoulder—plus a good chunk of safety fencing—were about sixty feet below us, balanced precariously on the slope. It must have been at least another hundred feet to the valley floor below.

A truck and two cars had been on the breakaway section when it fell. They lay jumbled on the makeshift ledge. Fluoro-jacketed rescue workers swarmed around them. I saw four people on stretchers and three zipped body bags.

"The doc wants him out of there yesterday," the former Marine was saying in a soft American drawl. "Day before that would be even better."

"Why not strap him in and drag him up the cliff wall," Riley suggested, frowning. "Bumpy ride but safer than me going down there that's for bloody sure."

The former Marine gave him the kind of stare that must have had raw recruits shivering in their boots. "We drag the kid up the cliff face and he loses the use of his legs."

Riley took a step closer to the edge, leaned out cautiously. As he did so, the former Marine seemed to notice me for the first time. His eyes narrowed. I gave him a nod of greeting he didn't return.

Riley stepped back between us. "Shit, boss. I got a half-load of cargo in the back of the old girl. She must weigh in at about eight thousand pounds. The downdraft alone could send the whole bloody lot heading for the bottom of the hill like a giant rock toboggan."

The former Marine raised an implacable eyebrow in a *So?* gesture.

Riley scowled. "And it's bloody close. I'll practically be weed whacking with the main rotor to get far enough in."

"Nothing you haven't done before," the former Marine said, and added, "By accident or design."

"What about winching him up?" I asked, nodding to the Bell.

"Ah." Riley looked embarrassed. "Local cops 'requisitioned' my winch yesterday. Bastards. I'm still trying to steal it back." He passed me a sour look and muttered, "Wouldn't have happened if we'd had decent security."

"Hey," I said, "yesterday I didn't even know I was coming."

The former Marine swung toward us in exasperation. He pointed a finger at me but his eyes were on Riley. "Excuse me," he said, "but who is she, exactly?"

"Stephens' replacement." Riley said with deliberation. He gave a leer. "Smaller muscles but bigger ti—"

"Yeah, I guess I can see that for myself," the former Marine cut in dryly. He held out his hand and we clasped briefly. He had a steel grip. "Joe Marcus."

"Charlie Fox."

He gave me a fractional nod then dismissed me from his mind and turned back to Riley. "You gonna get your ass back in that heap of junk, fly down there and pick up our casualty, or do I just kick you over the edge right now, save us all a heap of trouble?"

"Might cut out the middle man," Riley grumbled.

He took a final look over the precipice and spat for good measure, as if timing how long it would take the gob of saliva to reach the bottom.

"Ah, shit mate, why not?" he said at last. "Gotta die of something, right?" He started ambling toward the Bell, calling cheerfully over his shoulder, "Just in case the worst happens, I leave all my debts divided equally between my ex-wives."

I glanced across at Joe Marcus but clearly he had heard all this before. I turned and jogged for the helo. By the time Riley reached the cockpit I was already climbing in alongside him. He favoured me with a brief stare.

"You fed up with us already Charlie? Aiming to go home in a body bag yourself?"

I strapped in. "A Bell Twin Two-Twelve has a forty-eight foot rotor diameter," I said. "That ledge can't be more than twenty-five feet out from the cliff wall. If you're going to keep this thing out of the scrub you're going to need someone to spot for you."

For a moment he sat with his hands slack in his lap, then he shook his head and reached for the controls.

"Jeez," he said. "Stephens would have shit his pants."

"Yeah well, think of it as an added bonus," I said. "And that's on top of having bigger tits."

Five

WHEN IT MATTERED, Riley flew like an angel. I'd kind of hoped that might be the case.

If I'd been wrong we would both have been dead.

But he juggled the manual throttle, the cyclic and the collective, and the anti-torque pedals with a sure and delicate touch. He carefully sidled us, a few inches at a time, toward the wreckage on the fallen section of roadway while I hung out of my open cockpit door and guided him in.

Below us, the rescue team crouched away from the spinning rotors and sheltered the casualties with their own bodies. The protection they offered was more psychological than actual. If we'd touched the exposed cliff face with the rotor tips the resulting explosive disintegration would have probably wiped out everybody down there. As it was, the vicious downdraft beat them flat and grit-blasted them while it was about it.

As we crept closer I watched the longer fronds of stringy vegetation clinging to the rock wall until they became whipped into frenzy by the displaced air. The Bell rocked and plunged like a small boat caught in a cross-current, dipping the main rotors perilously close to the cliff with every jagged roll.

"Is this as good as it gets?" I demanded.

"You think you can do better, sweetheart, you're welcome to give it a shot," Riley managed from between clenched teeth. "I'm losing half my bloody lift over the outboard side. Now then, hang about."

His hands shifted. The Bell gave a lurch and then steadied with the pilot's side of the helo maybe a foot lower. Instead of the aircraft having to cope with a long drop on one side and a very short one on the other, the space underneath us was more equalised. He feathered the controls just enough to hold station and grinned at me. It wasn't exactly glass-like, but it was a big improvement.

"Hey, would you look at that? Piece o' cake."

I hauled myself back into the door aperture and watched the rotors. The angle opened up room for us to edge another vital couple of feet closer.

"OK, that's close enough!" I ordered. The skid on my side was directly overhanging the mangled guard rail that had dropped, as one lump, with the rest of the section of road.

I straightened back into my seat, wedging the door ajar with my knee, and glanced at Riley. "Can you keep it steady right there?"

"'Course, mate." The Aussie even managed to sound a little bored. "There's not a fart of wind. Long as it stays that way, no worries."

"Good," I said. "Because if I can get down there in one piece, chances are we can get the casualty back the same way."

I pulled off my headset without waiting for his comments, shoved open the door again and got out.

I tried not to think about the hundred feet of nothing beneath me as I clambered onto the skid and used the guard rail as a stepping stone before jumping down onto the cracked concrete. And all the while I made sure to keep my head low.

A slim dark-haired woman half rose to meet me. Her face was perfectly calm, as if total strangers walked out of mid-air helicopters in front of her every day of the week.

"Doc?" I guessed, shouting to be heard. She nodded. "This is close as we get. Where's your patient?"

She beckoned. Four people hurried forward carrying a stretcher between them. The boy strapped onto the stretcher was wearing a surgical collar to stabilise his neck. He looked no more than seventeen. His eyes were closed and there was a mess of blood tangling his hair. Another rescue worker jogged alongside the stretcher carrying a drip that was plugged into his arm, and pumping the resus bag covering his nose and mouth.

"'Ow do you propose we do this?" the doctor asked. She had a heavy accent I couldn't place with all the background noise.

"Bloody carefully," I said. "We'll slide him up and in across the cargo bay. I'll go first. Be ready."

She nodded again without argument. I turned back to the hovering Bell. From the ground, getting back into it seemed a hell of a lot more difficult than getting out had done. The vicious downdraft buffeted me and I couldn't help the horrible feeling that the rotors were skimming my hair the same way as that vegetation.

I took a deep breath and leapt for the guard rail and the skid at the same time. I'd been aiming for the rear door but as I landed the helicopter gave a sudden outward lurch. My foot slipped off the railing. I hurled myself forward, grabbing messily for the cockpit door handle instead, wrenching it open. I tumbled back inside with my heart hammering against my ribs so loud it must have drowned out the noise of the engines.

Riley sat slumped and impassive in the pilot's seat. Relief made me grin stupidly at him. "Miss me?"

Without waiting for an answer I squeezed between the front seats, staggered into the rear and tugged the cliff-side door open. It slid back alongside the fuselage.

As soon as I'd done so the dark-haired doctor climbed up coolly onto the guard rail and put her hand out without waiting to be invited. I hastily clasped it and yanked her inside. In contrast with my own graceless efforts she landed with the ease of a dancer. Bitch.

The front two stretcher-bearers lifted one end high enough to reach the cargo deck and everybody pushed. The doc and I took hold and between us, with amazingly little further drama, we hauled the stretcher on board. I slammed the door shut again.

Riley didn't need any further signal, moving away instantly.

The doctor nodded to me just once, then reached for a headset and gave Riley instructions about which medical centre to head for. As she spoke she checked the boy's airway and worked the resus bag to keep him breathing. I hung the saline pouch feeding his drip line high enough not to become a drain instead and strapped down the stretcher.

When I was done I threaded my way to my front seat again and stuck my own headset back on. Riley flicked me a glance that was suddenly serious.

"Nice going, Charlie," he said. "Thought I'd lost you for a moment there."

"Yeah," I agreed. "You'll have to try a damn sight harder next time."

Just for a second he looked startled but then he grinned at me. "No way would old Stevo have given that a go."

"Thanks," I said. I re-fastened my belts, although after the last ten minutes it seemed an oddly redundant gesture. "You never did tell me what happened to him."

"He got careless," Riley said. "And then he got unlucky."

Six

THE DOCTOR'S NAME was Alexandria Bertrand and the accent I hadn't been able to discern amid all the other distractions turned out to be French. She was a highly regarded trauma specialist who'd jacked in her career at one of the best hospitals in Paris and done five years with *Médecins Sans Frontières* before joining R&R. So I surmised she'd seen the very worst people could do to each other anywhere TripAdvisor warned you not to go.

She was also a qualified forensic pathologist and as soon as the rescue efforts started to scale down she would begin the heartbreaking and laborious task of identifying the dead. Maybe she had more affinity with them than the living. She certainly didn't impress me with her bedside manner. But, having a top-class surgeon for a father I was only too familiar with that haughty clinical demeanour.

I found out most of her background from staff at the medical centre where we transported the injured boy from the roadway collapse. The centre was located in an area of the city least affected by the quake, although the sheer numbers of incoming casualties meant most of the injured were going through military-style triage and then being treated in a makeshift field hospital. Requisitioned tents and marquees stretched out across the parking areas.

Dr Bertrand saw her patient into the care of the surgical team and handed him over with a concise recitation of his injuries and the treatment he'd received so far. There was too much blood on his forehead for her to write the traditional 'M' there to indicate she'd given him a hefty dose of morphine and she made a pain of herself insisting they make proper note of it.

"I 'ave risked too much to bring this boy 'ere," she told them in that icily exotic voice, "only for you to overdose 'im on the operating table."

"I *have* risked…"

So, not only a complete lack of bedside manner, but no concept of being a team player either.

She and my father would have got on like a house on fire.

As they hurriedly wheeled the boy away to pre-op she peeled off her latex gloves and dropped them into the nearest waste bin. There was a symbolic finality to the act, a washing of hands.

Then she turned to me. I expected some form of greeting but instead she gave me a swift cool appraisal and asked, "Where is Riley? I must get back to my work."

I jerked my head toward the landing area nearby where we'd just set down. "Offloading medical supplies."

"Then tell 'im to 'urry," she responded, and swept out past me.

"Yes ma'am," I said under my breath. "And it's a pleasure to be working with you, too…"

It wasn't until we were in the air again twenty minutes later that she deigned to offer me her full attention. We were travelling in the rear of the helicopter on flip-down seats facing each other, so it was harder for her to avoid it.

Riley was left to his own devices in the cockpit. He seemed put out that he could no longer play the inept rookie with me, and as a result he flew a smooth straight course, forsaking drama as well as conversation. Maybe it was simply the dampening effect Dr Bertrand had on him.

Without its cargo the interior of the Bell seemed vast. The empty space beat with reflected flight noise like a giant drum.

"So, Charlie," she said via the headsets we both wore, curling my name into something more than it was, "why are you 'ere?"

I had my official story down pat. "To advise your team on personal safety, minimise risk, protect you if necessary, help out where I can."

"That is not what I meant." She frowned. "But your actions out there today," she went on, her fingers making a small gesture to indicate the helicopter and all that had gone into the rescue, "were they safe—or advisable?"

"I think that falls under both protecting you *and* helping out."

"But you did not seem to give much regard to your own safety. 'Ow can we be sure you will give regard to ours?"

"I said *minimise* risk. I know I can't eliminate it entirely, so my job is to put myself between you and whatever hazards I can, but still allow you the freedom to do your work," I said. I paused. "I understand you lost a team member recently. I'm sorry. Please be assured I will do everything I can not to let that happen again."

"Thank you." She favoured me with a vaguely regal nod. "I confess that I did not like Kyle Stephens, but in most ways 'e was a professional and I could at least admire that."

"Why didn't you like him?"

She gave me a slow blink, almost in surprise that I had the temerity to ask.

"'E did not think much of women," she said at last.

"Can I ask...what happened to him?"

She stiffened. "Why do you ask?"

"I try to learn from past mistakes in order to avoid repeating them. Other people's as well as my own."

"It was...'e did not..." She gave a growl of frustration and tried again: "Natural disasters are often followed by great lawlessness...people who wish to take advantage of the situation for their own gain. This can make such places very dangerous, as Monsieur Stephens found out to 'is cost."

"Dangerous how?" I persisted.

She flashed me a quick look of irritation. "We were in an area of Colombia where the rule of law is somewhat... tenuous," she said at last. "The local guerrilla fighters were determined to come in and take what they wanted—including our equipment and supplies. We needed time to make a successful evacuation." She shrugged. "Perhaps 'e should 'ave advised us to move out sooner. 'E paid the price for that oversight."

All of which was precisely no help whatsoever towards finding out what actually caused the death of my predecessor.

And no help either towards planning how best to avoid following in his footsteps.

Seven

THE DEAD LAY IN ROWS in a temporary mortuary established at an army base about ten klicks from the capital.

In the weird way of earthquakes, while some areas were totally destroyed this whole place had escaped totally unscathed. Everyone fervently hoped it would stay that way. Even so, whenever an aftershock hit there was a fractional pause before they carried on. Outside, there was the constant rumble of engines from the line of commandeered refrigeration trucks being used for storage.

Dr Bertrand briefly explained the cataloguing system used for each victim as they were brought in. Every piece of clothing and personal items had to be removed, photographed and bagged.

She seemed to take it for granted that I wouldn't freak out in close proximity to so many corpses. Particularly ones who had not exactly died peacefully in their sleep. Her only concern was whether I could be trusted to operate a camera with enough skill to be useful.

"This is not in my brief," I pointed out. "Wouldn't I be more—?"

"Tomorrow—maybe," she interrupted, thrusting a Canon digital SLR and a clipboard into my hands. "But the teams are already scattered across the city. For now you are more use 'ere."

I shrugged. "Where do I start?"

And so I began. The quake had been no respecter of age, race or social status—an equal-opportunity killer. That first day I listed and photographed toys found clutched in the hands of children, lavish rings from well-manicured fingers, and the rags of the homeless.

I was handed all these possessions to arrange and record as they were stripped from the bodies. In some cases blood and other debris had to be cleaned from them first.

"We try to make an initial identification from family or friends recognising the property found with the victim," I was told by the girl I was working with. She introduced herself too fast for me to catch her name and there never seemed to be opportunity to ask a second time.

The level of concentration I felt compelled to maintain in order to give these people the respect they deserved made it an engrossing but dismal task.

There were four DVI teams—Disaster Victim Identification—from different countries working alongside each other. Apart from the murmuring of the pathologists dictating their observations and the occasional rapid rattle of a bone saw, the only sounds were the muted pop of camera flashes and the flutter of Canon motorwinds.

No chatter, no jokes, no music.

The Japanese team, so experienced in dealing with situations like this, held a sombre minute's silence before starting on each new victim. An overwhelming sense of sadness pervaded the place. By the time I'd been there a couple of hours I was mentally and emotionally flattened.

"Charlie." Dr Bertrand's voice, loud and unexpected, made me jump. "I need you over 'ere."

I turned, saw the young guy who'd been photographing for her stumbling away with his shoulders hunched.

"'E is too tired to work efficiently," Dr Bertrand said, following my gaze. "I 'ave sent 'im to get some rest, and so I must make do with you."

I bit back my instinctive sarcastic comment and said instead, "What do you need?"

She laid a hand on the naked thigh of the overweight middle-aged male cadaver on her table, like a butcher contemplating which cut to take from a side of pig.

"This man 'as an artificial 'ip," she began.

"Which will have a unique serial number tied to the patient who received it."

She gave me a small sideways glance but stopped short of actual praise.

"I will, of course, need to expose that area of the implant for you to document," she warned.

"Of course," I repeated blandly.

I had seen the dead up close before. In fact I had been the cause of death more times than was probably good for my eternal soul. And once I watched my father carry out an emergency procedure to clamp a man's severed brachial artery by the side of a road, armed with no more than a Swiss Army knife and the rusty toolkit from a Ford pickup truck.

But I had never witnessed such a swift and brutal partial dismemberment as Alexandria Bertrand performed. Her incisions were precise and practical, without a wasted stroke or hesitation. The image of her as a butcher returned as she peeled back the dead man's skin and flesh with no more drama than if she'd been boning a joint of meat for Sunday lunch. Then she stepped back with an impatient flick of her fingers.

"There. Be sure it is entirely visible and in sharp focus."

I snapped away and checked the results on the view screen at the back of the camera, zooming in as far as it would allow. But when I offered to show the good doctor she waved me away. It brought to mind generals who give orders and expect them to be carried out without question, but who would never lower themselves far enough to actually check.

We worked on into the evening. By then I had confirmed my first impression of Dr Bertrand. She was tireless, ruthless and humourless. But bloody hell she was good at her job.

Exactly the same qualities were much admired in contract killers.

"Hey, Al!" called a voice from the doorway.

My head jerked up and I realised Dr Bertrand and I were the only two people left in the mortuary amid a sea of empty stainless steel tables.

The former Marine, Joe Marcus weaved his way between them. He had exchanged his coveralls for light-weight trousers and a cotton shirt but everything about him carried the authority of rank.

"Clear up and give the new kid a break," he said. "Chow time."

Dr Bertrand let out her breath and frowned as if considering whether or not to comply. The fact he'd called her "Al" didn't seem to cause a flicker. Marcus reached us and stood silently across the other side of our work station. She had just finished with the burned body of an old woman and I had carefully put all her documented charred belongings back into a labelled archive box and shelved it in the ante room next door while she completed her notes.

From that point of view Marcus's timing was excellent. It didn't stop Dr Bertrand having a short stare-out competition with him, though. I reckoned they were fairly evenly matched, but in the end the former Marine beat her on points.

"You're only as good as the most exhausted member of your unit," he said.

I would have argued about that, but realised it would not do me any favours.

"OK," Dr Bertrand said at last. She peeled off her gloves and dropped them into a flip-top bin, in the same way she'd done earlier at the medical centre after we'd delivered the boy from the roadside. I followed suit. Marcus nodded at her capitulation.

At the doorway she stopped and looked back almost longingly.

"Dead is dead. Another few hours isn't gonna make any difference to them," Marcus said quietly. "But it will to you."

She switched off the light without replying and we stepped outside into the humid wash of evening.

While Dr Bertrand locked up Joe Marcus shifted his eyes to me.

"You were lucky out there today," he said. "Nice reflexes."

For a moment I went blank on his meaning then realised he was talking about that slip as I'd jumped for the helicopter. The rescue on the cliffside seemed to have taken place days ago.

"Yeah well," I said with a smile, "I told Riley he'd have to try harder than that if he wanted to get rid of me."

His eyes narrowed and I didn't miss the quick look that Dr Bertrand flicked in his direction. And in that instant I had sudden flash-recall of launching myself for the Bell, of the helo jinking away from me at exactly the wrong moment.

Or had it been exactly the *right* moment?

Not enough to appear deliberate—just a correction for an unexpected gust of wind buffeting the aircraft. But coming after Riley had stated there was "not a fart" of a breeze, even allowing for the difficult angle, it sent a shiver of delayed reaction along every nerve.

And when I met Joe Marcus's gaze I saw that he either knew anyway or he'd already worked it out. He stared back at me steadily.

I'd thought Dr Bertrand was a cold one, but I realised that he was infinitely colder.

"Let us eat," she said abruptly. "There is still much work to do."

She strode away along a narrow path bordered by whitewashed stones. Marcus indicated I should go before him with a sweep of his arm. Good manners precluded my refusal, but I found I didn't like him walking behind me.

I'd come here looking for a potential killer.

Instead I'd found three.

Eight

ONLY A FEW HOURS before I boarded that Hercules I'd never heard of an outfit called Rescue & Recovery International. Nor had I ever crossed paths with a former US Army Ranger called Kyle Stephens. The fact that he was dead was of little interest to me.

I had other things on my mind.

Foremost of these worries was the state of my relationship with Sean Meyer. Sean had been my training instructor during my short and bitterly inglorious military career. The toughest of a tough bunch, he was the one who had goaded me towards excellence. And just when I thought he was the coldest bastard I'd ever encountered, he confounded me by offering a glimpse of his human side that provoked an incendiary desire.

Our affair while we were still in uniform was short-lived, illicit, and ultimately doomed not only to failure but to personal and professional ruin for both of us.

I never would have dreamed back then that Sean and I would reconnect, or would end up living together in New York working for Parker Armstrong's prestigious close-protection agency. We'd certainly had our share of high points, but there had been some equally stunning blows as well.

The previous winter I nearly lost him for good. For more than three months I pilgrimaged daily to his bedside while he lay in a coma and on some subconscious level made up his mind between holding on and letting go.

And during all that time I loved him and hated him in equal measure.

In the end my prayers were answered but with a sick twist neither of us could have prepared for. We came back to each other changed from who we were—and not for the better. Just when I finally became more like Sean—more like the old Sean *wanted* me to be—he became less like himself.

Everyone from the neurosurgeon who dug the fragments of skull out of his brain, to the coma specialists and psychologists, had warned us he might be different afterwards. *If* he lived.

The one thing I clung to was that if he made it back then the bond between us was strong enough to cope with whatever might follow. In the event, I found myself devastated by his sudden unexpected enmity towards me. For someone in a profession that stands or falls by its anticipation of every obstacle, I admit *that* one took me completely by surprise.

We still shared the Upper East Side apartment Parker had arranged for us as part of our relocation deal, but I moved my things into the second bedroom. At first this was a temporary measure while Sean acclimatised to the fact we were a couple. His last waking memory of me was as someone he despised.

As is always the way with temporary measures, the move soon became permanent. But it also seemed to ease the tension between us. He took some tentative steps toward me and I thought, finally, we might be making progress.

And then it all changed again.

The day that eight-point-six earthquake hit I sat watching the news coverage and teetering on the cusp of melancholy. And that's when Parker Armstrong rang me.

"Charlie!" he greeted. There was surprise in his voice, as if he hadn't expected to catch me at home when he knew that's where I'd be. "How you doing?"

"I'm fine."

He let the lie pass, said instead, "I have a client coming in at three this afternoon. I'd like for you to be here, meet with them."

I poked my brain doggedly into work mode. "Is this a solo job or part of a full detail?"

Parker hesitated. "Not exactly either," he said. "Best if the client explains it to you herself."

"OK, so what's the threat?" The question lacked finesse, but hell—people didn't hire Armstrong-Meyer unless they needed protecting from something bad.

"Your guess is as good as mine," he said, not sounding at all fazed.

I felt my eyebrows rise. Parker was usually meticulous. He possessed a wariness born of long experience at the sharp end of close-protection work. He did not normally offer his services—or those of his operatives—on such an open-ended basis.

In spite of myself, I was intrigued. And almost anything was better than this frantic inactivity.

"OK," I said. "I'll be there."

I made sure I reached the midtown offices of the Armstrong-Meyer agency a good half an hour before the appointed time. Excessive perhaps, but Parker always stressed that we were there to wait on our clients, not the other way around.

As it was, I was told to go right in as soon as I stepped out of the lift into the marble-tiled lobby. The Armstrong-Meyer nameplate was still displayed behind the reception desk. I wondered how long Parker could continue to keep Sean as a full partner when he no longer played an active role.

I knocked briefly and opened the door to Parker's office. His domain occupied a corner of the building. It had a fabulous view out over the Manhattan skyline but I didn't get chance to admire it.

Parker was not alone, I saw immediately. There was a woman with him who was sitting in one of the low client chairs that bracketed a coffee table in the centre of the room. She was in her forties and the best word to describe her was sleek.

She was dressed with a careless elegance only the long-term wealthy ever truly manage well. I couldn't pull it off with a gun to my head. What little jewellery she wore was antique and expensive without being gaudy. Her hair and nails were flawless. And she was a redhead—one of Parker's weaknesses.

My boss was standing behind his desk, leaning both fists onto the polished surface, his arms braced. His head came up sharply when I entered.

For a horrible moment I thought I'd walked in on a situation that was personal rather than professional. There was definitely something going on even if I couldn't put my finger on what. I heard the tension fizzing in the air and saw the flash of stubbornness in the woman's eyes. Eyes that widened when I walked in on them.

I froze with one hand on the door handle.

"I was told you were ready for me, sir," I said quickly, keeping it formal just in case. "But I can come back later if you're—"

"No, no, come on in," Parker said. He straightened and lifting a shoulder as if to ease the tension in his neck. "Mrs

Hamilton," he went on, "this is the operative we've been discussing—Charlie Fox."

I shut the door and came forward. Mrs Hamilton rose to meet me, neatly pushing aside all appearance of irritation, and gave me the kind of smile that makes you believe it really *is* a pleasure. Nevertheless, I caught the way her eyes slid questioningly to his and the bland look he passed her in reply.

I pretended not to notice, taking a seat opposite and crossing my legs. I was glad I'd taken the time to put on a decent black suit for the occasion. What made me less happy was the fact I'd chosen to wear an open-necked shirt with it.

The old scar around the base of my throat had faded to a thin line that didn't tan well. I was still touchy about it even though it was only noticeable if you knew to look— and for some reason Mrs Hamilton seemed to know. I returned her gaze evenly. She flushed slightly and glanced away.

Parker, who'd missed nothing of this, gave her a brief reassuring smile.

"Thanks for coming in at such short notice, Charlie, but we have something of a time-sensitive situation."

"No problem," I said. "What's the brief?"

He nodded to Mrs Hamilton. "If you'd care to fill Charlie in on some of the background?"

Again there was more in the tone than the words but the redhead simply gave a reluctant nod.

"I guess I ought to tell you right away that I am finding it hard to maintain a level of emotional detachment from all this," she said.

Most clients who came to us suffered the same problem, but to have her admit it up front was refreshing.

She took a deep breath. "My husband died in the Tōhoku earthquake in Japan," she said. "He was over there on business, decided to take an extra day or two at the end of his trip to see the sights, and as a result he became one of nearly twenty-five thousand dead, injured or missing."

I did a quick mental calculation and worked out the Tōhoku earthquake was several years previously. Not long enough to sate her grief, clearly, but enough to dull the pain just a little.

"I'm very sorry for your loss," I murmured.

She nodded her acknowledgement, went on. "He was in the hotel restaurant when the building simply ... came down around him, trapped him in the rubble. Afterward, well—" she turned diffident, "—they said he might have survived if help had gotten to him sooner."

I said nothing. Slow deaths are harder to bear, I knew, than if he'd been killed instantly.

Instead, it was Parker who said, "Mrs Hamilton is now a major donor supporting an outfit called Rescue & Recovery International."

I felt my lips try to quirk inappropriately upwards and controlled them only with effort. Parker's face showed no inner amusement. Had he never watched the puppet *Thunderbirds* series as a kid? The Tracy family living on their private island and running International Rescue on the side?

"Yes," Mrs Hamilton said, reading me with uncanny accuracy. "I guess that makes me Lady Penelope, doesn't it?"

I let go and grinned at her. "And not forgetting her trusty butler-turned-chauffeur."

"Of course!" Her eyes flew to my boss. "His name was Parker."

Parker's face remained impassive. I suppose one of us had to behave like a grownup.

"And you have concerns with this Rescue & Recovery?" I asked. I couldn't bring myself to include the "International" part.

"Yes," she agreed, her eyes on my boss.

Parker said, "Rescue & Recovery—they're known as R&R—was formed as an emergency response team shortly after that Japanese quake in two-thousand-ten. Their mission statement is to provide rapid emergency assistance on the ground, anywhere in the world, twenty-four/seven, three-sixty-five days a year."

I nodded. All very interesting but so far I didn't see where I came in. I silently indicated this to Parker with a face that asked, *So?*

"They go into areas which, by their very nature, are experiencing upheaval and a degree of civil unrest. It is a requirement of their insurance to have a security advisor on board. Until three weeks ago that was a guy called Kyle Stephens."

He lifted a manila folder from his desk and held it out to me. I flipped it open and saw a head and shoulders shot of a thickset man with a bull neck and a nose that had seen some action. He was uniformed in the mug shot. I recognised the red lightning streak cap badge of the US Army Rangers.

"Is there a problem with Stephens?" I asked, skimming his impressive résumé. "He looks like an ideal man for the job."

"He's dead."

I blinked. "How?"

"That rather seems to be the question," Mrs Hamilton said. She sighed. "Three weeks ago they were in South America. Mudslides in Colombia. Four hundred dead—many of them children. Two schools were destroyed. It was a nightmare, not just the continuing heavy rains but increased guerrilla activity in the area causing havoc as well. It was dangerous in many ways but that's all part of the job."

I heard an edge to her voice and wondered who she was trying to convince. I said nothing but Parker gave her an encouraging nod. Her answering smile was grateful but there was still something slightly strained between them. I wondered again what they'd been arguing about before my arrival.

"At first it all seemed normal—as normal as their work ever gets. They took the rescue operation as far as they could and moved on to recovering the bodies." She shook her head. "All those children. It was heartbreaking."

"I read the reports," Parker said gently. "It was a tragedy."

"And the next thing I know I get a call on the sat-phone from the team leader, Joe Marcus. Anyhow, Joe tells me Kyle has 'met with an accident'."

"Did he say what kind of an accident?"

"No, but it wasn't *what* he said, it was the *way* he said it. It's hard to explain. Joe can be a tough man to read but there was just too much anger."

"That wouldn't be unusual," Parker pointed out. "Losing somebody you feel responsible for can make you...rage."

He didn't look at me as he spoke. I didn't look at him either.

"But it was as though he was angry *with* Kyle, not because of something that happened *to* him," Mrs Hamilton said. "It was as though Joe was taking it person-ally somehow."

"Same rule applies," I said. "If someone dies because they made a mistake—especially a one-off stupid mistake—that would do it, too."

"Funny." She eyed us both. "When I pressed Joe about it later, that's exactly what he said."

"But?" I put in, because in situations like these there's always a "but".

Mrs Hamilton paused. She uncrossed and re-crossed her elegant legs. Eventually she said, "Do you trust your instincts, Miss Fox—when it comes to people, I mean?"

"Mostly," I said, because there were times when my instincts had let me down big time. And other times when

I'd refused to listen to my internal warning system. Usually to my cost.

She heard all that in my one-word answer, smiled and said, "Well then, if you 'mostly' trust your instincts, do you then follow up on them, or do you let it slide?"

It was a good point. I couldn't come back with anything except agreement. I shrugged.

"All right," I said. "What does your instinct tell you about Kyle Stephens?"

She hesitated again, because now we were drifting from facts into feelings. She glanced at Parker again for support.

"That I might have gotten him killed."

"It was brought to Mrs Hamilton's attention that there had been a number of *incidents* that coincide with the arrival on scene of R&R's people," Parker said.

"What kind of 'incidents'?" I asked, echoing his emphasis. "You mean threats against them?"

Parker shook his head. "Thefts," he said bluntly.

Mrs Hamilton's body shifted in protest. "In the confusion following the kind of natural disasters they deal with, it's easy for things to be…lost, but this is more than that," she said, her voice hollow. "It's deliberate, organised theft, and I won't have any part in it."

"What proof do you have that anyone who works for R&R is involved?" I asked.

"An anonymous tip, delivered via a third party I knew slightly," she said. "A warning to…disassociate myself before it becomes a scandal."

"Which you're reluctant to do," I surmised.

"Wouldn't you be?" she demanded. "Whatever *else* they may be up to, my team does amazing work, locating and rescuing the injured and then recovering, identifying and reconciling the dead. Rebuilding shattered infrastructure. My people bring hope and help and closure to thousands—"

My team, I thought. *My people...*

"I realise that and I do entirely appreciate your dilemma," Parker said soothingly, cutting her off before she could get into her stride.

"No, you don't," she shot back. "You don't appreciate just how *guilty* I feel."

That brought both of us up short. I flicked my eyes to Parker's.

"Mrs Hamilton," he said carefully, "what exactly do you have to feel guilty about?"

But she wouldn't look at either of us. "Kyle was there for security. Not only to keep the team safe but to help maintain law and order. So I asked him to...look into what I'd heard," she said, speaking low. "And now he's dead."

"And you feel his death was a little too convenient?"

"Isn't it?" Anger pulsed through her voice. "Either it's a coincidence and he was just plain unlucky, or he was silenced. Silenced because of something *I* asked him to do," she said. "I can't take the not knowing. It's destroying my faith in R&R and the work they do. How can I be proud of something that might be so tainted? To steal from the dead, the dying or the injured. It's a desecration."

"Which is why I propose sending in Charlie," Parker said. "To put your mind at rest."

She made a brief gesture of frustration with her hands, and I realised this was probably the point where I'd come in.

"I'm sorry, Miss Fox—Charlie," she said. "I mean no offence, but Kyle Stephens was a decorated veteran of two Gulf Wars and Afghanistan, and yet still he ended up dead. And now Mr Armstrong wants to send in a young woman who can hardly have the same kind of experience or—"

"One of Charlie's many strengths is the fact people woefully underestimate her abilities," Parker said. "Trust me, she is more than capable of handling herself. If she wasn't, do you honestly believe I'd propose sending her?"

Mrs Hamilton's eyes skated over me. They lingered again on the scar at my throat and I couldn't quite decide if the sight of it reassured her or not. She bit her lower lip.

"It's very short notice," she said, as if that final point might dissuade me.

I was wearing the TAG Heuer wristwatch Sean had given me as a 'welcome to New York' gift shortly after we arrived. I checked it and did some fast mental calculations. Not for the first time since some bastard ran my Buell Firebolt off the road I cursed the fact I had yet to replace the bike. It would have halved my travel time.

"I keep a go-bag ready packed at home," I said. "I can be ready to leave in less than an hour."

Mrs Hamilton was silent for maybe half a minute. We let the silence run.

Eventually she sighed and got to her feet. "All right," she said, checking her own watch. "An hour? That's good, because the next transport plane out is due to leave the Air Cargo centre at JFK a little over three hours from now."

I smiled. "Should give me plenty of time then."

Parker ran me out to the airport himself, despite my protests. I appreciated the ride, but if he played personal chauffeur for me too often I was going to start getting knowing leers from the other guys and comments about how the boss was trying to get into my pants.

The problem was they wouldn't have been far wrong.

Not that Parker would ever be quite so crass, but he'd shown beyond any doubt that it would only take the slightest encouragement from me to turn our relationship into something much more personal.

He wanted me, maybe even loved me. And part of me recognised that it would have been such an easy step to take.

It would also have been totally wrong for both of us.

"Any hunches, doubts, suspicions, you call me, a-sap," he ordered as he dropped me off outside a hanger belonging to the freight company that was co-ordinating the latest earthquake relief supplies. "And Charlie—watch your six."

"I will," I said, answering both questions. I grabbed my bag from the footwell and climbed out, then paused while the howl of a jet powering through take-off made speech temporarily impossible. Then I said, "And if you hear anything from Sean...?"

His face hardened. "I've got people working on it. *When* we find him—not *if*—I'll call you," he promised. "Just as fast."

Nine

THE MORNING AFTER MY ARRIVAL I met the final two regular members of what Mrs Hamilton had described as "the core team" that made up R&R. A thin waiflike girl and a leggy blonde bitch.

As I arrived at the mess hall where non-stop breakfast was being served, Joe Marcus was just leaving. We did the usual dance in the doorway before he stepped back and beckoned me through with a slightly impatient jerk of his head.

"You'll be working with Hope this morning. Girl over by the far wall—looks like she hasn't eaten for a month and won't eat for another," he said by way of description. "That's Hope Tyler. Don't let the appearance fool you. She's the best I've seen in a long time. But you'll get to judge that for yourself later."

I followed his eyeline and saw a girl whose youth was exaggerated by her thinness. She was all bones and sharp angles. In view of Marcus's description I eyed the way she was tucking into the typical carb-laden stodge being provided by the army camp's catering corps and concluded she had a lightning metabolism, hollow legs, or a tapeworm.

The leggy blonde bitch sat alongside her.

The bitch's name was Lemon. She was a four-year-old yellow Labrador retriever possessed of an extremely sensitive nose and the most expressive eyebrows I'd ever seen on a dog.

I loaded up my own tray with food before I went over to introduce myself. I'd eaten in hundreds of such places during my time in uniform. The country, climate and cap badges might be different but the smell remained exactly the same.

As I approached the dog sidled in and leaned heavily against my thigh. Normal rules about keeping animals and food separated did not apply in the military. If you had a dog in your unit capable of sniffing out Improvised Explosive Devices, you kept it close at all times.

"Hello, and what do you want, hmm?" I murmured. "Yeah, like I couldn't guess."

The yellow Lab beat her frantic tail against my knees while she trampled on my feet. It was my most enthusiastic reception so far.

When that didn't get the dog the attention she wanted, she gave a couple of restrained barks and bounced stiff-legged off the floor a few times. I reckoned she was just trying to take a sneaky look at what was on my tray.

"Lemon, leave her alone!" Hope said, lifting her eyes from her plate for the first time. "Cor, sorry about that. If she's not wearing her harness she thinks she don't have to listen to a word I say. Lemon!"

Her accent was British, from an indeterminate mixture of regions with maybe a hint of south London at the base of it. I threaded my way towards her between the tables with the dog lurking round my heels.

"Better than the other way around I suppose. And it's no problem—I like dogs." I looked down at Lemon who had the most amazing green eyes. She put her head on one side appealingly as she tried to persuade me that she was in danger of imminent starvation unless I slipped her half my food. "Not a chance," I told her. "This bacon may need carbon dating but it's all mine."

Hope laughed. "Oh, she's got your number all right, Lem," she told the dog, rubbing the gold-tipped ears.

"Too right," I agreed. "Mind if I join you?"

"Make yourself at home," Hope said. "Always nice to come across a fellow Brit."

She had finished shovelling down her fry-up and now she straightened, wiping her mouth almost delicately before reaching for her mug. From the colour and smell, it was filled with the thick strong army tea I remembered so well and disliked so much. Like I said—some things never change.

"Joe Marcus pointed you out to me," I said once I'd unloaded my tray. I stuck out my hand. "I'm Charlie Fox. Apparently we're working together today."

Hope didn't respond right away. She just sat and stared at me with a strange look on her face as if I'd said something that didn't quite compute.

As if sensing the awkward moment developing, Lemon stuck her snout under the edge of Hope's elbow and turfed it upwards, splashing lukewarm tea all over the surface of the trestle table.

Hope protested with a cry of, "Oh, *Lemon!*" But she was laughing as she said it.

By the time we'd mopped up, and one of the squaddies had smilingly brought her a replacement mug of tea, the tension had passed. Lemon sank onto her haunches and continued to dust the floor with her tail, but more half-heartedly now. Her soulful eyes switched back and forth between the two of us like a spectator at a tennis match.

"I don't believe it," Hope said then. "When Riley said he was off to pick up the new bloke at the airport yesterday I thought, well, that you'd *be* a bloke."

She rested her elbows on the trestle table and held the mug up close to her lips. The fingernails on her skinny fingers were bitten down so far past the quick it made me wince.

"Yeah," I said. "I get that a lot."

"So you've taken over from Kyle Stephens full time then, eh?"

I shook my head. "Just until they can sort out someone permanent," I said.

She looked disappointed. "Oh, would'a been nice to have another girl to hang out with," she said. "Dr B—Dr Bertrand—well, she doesn't hang out much."

"I can imagine," I said. "We met yesterday. The frostbite hasn't started to heal yet."

Hope hid a giggle behind her mug, watching me with one bright eye over the top. "She's all right once you get to know her," she said, and seemed to surprise herself with that statement.

"How long have you been with R&R?"

"About three months," Hope said. "Only got the job 'cos I pestered 'em non-stop until they'd give us a trial." She put a hand on top of the dog's head and smoothed her fur. "Soon showed 'em though, Lem, didn't we? Soon showed 'em, girl." She looked up, a fierce pride bringing colour to her pale cheeks. "She's the best search and rescue dog ever."

Her vehemence made me wary.

"Well, apparently I'm partnering you this morning, so I'll get the chance to see her in action," I said. "I'm looking forward to it."

Lemon edged her muzzle onto the tabletop. Her eyes really were beautiful, a fact which she was only too well aware of. She fixed them on my plate and let out a gusty sigh.

"Had one of the local cops out with us yesterday," Hope said. "But they're spread so thin that if they get a call they naff off and we're all on our tod."

"Well I promise not to naff off and leave you."

"Great," she said and lowered her voice a little. "Gets a bit creepy out there sometimes. Puts the wind right up us, doesn't it, Lem?"

The dog's eyebrows rose in response. She gave another exaggerated sigh and licked her lips. I did my best to ignore her.

"Have you had any trouble?"

Hope lifted a bony shoulder. "Not as yet but it's coming. Soon as people's stocks run out and they gotta start scavenging, that's when things can get a bit hairy. And we tend to work on our own, y'see. No point in having a crowd of diggers standing around with their thumbs up their backsides until Lem's found something for 'em to dig up, is there girl?"

I assumed that last question was either rhetorical or aimed at the yellow Lab anyway. Hope didn't strike me as an ideal dog handler. Her movements were too quick and nervy. I would have thought she'd turn even the most placid animal into a twitching wreck inside the first week.

Lemon rolled her eyes in my direction causing her eyebrows to bob again. It was hard not to paint human emotions onto the gesture, as if she'd sensed my doubts.

"You worked with Kyle Stephens quite a bit then?" I asked casually.

Hope stilled. Lemon cocked her head on one side, her ears raised in query. Hope stroked her until she subsided, then mumbled, "Yeah, sometimes."

"Do you know what happened to him?" I asked. I dropped my voice to match her earlier conspiratorial level and pushed my luck. "I mean, I know he died but nobody seems to want to say how and if it's something I need to know about—so I can try to stop the same thing happening again—"

"It won't!" Hope blurted. She checked to see who might have overheard but the mess hall was busy, the level of background conversation and clatter high enough to conceal her outburst. "It won't," she repeated more quietly. "Joe told him not to but he did it anyway."

I had to lean in to hear her words. "Joe told him not to do what?"

She glanced at me quickly then, as if aware she'd already said too much. "Go into buildings that was unsafe," she said hurriedly. "That's what I heard. Joe's an engineer so he knows all about stuff like that, but Kyle didn't do what Joe told him and he got himself killed for it."

She got up, almost leapt to her feet. "I gotta go get sorted," she said. "I'll pick up our search grid and meet you out front in twenty minutes, yeah?"

And she scurried off without waiting for a reply. Lemon let her go. The dog had her head back glued to the tabletop near my plate.

My turn to sigh. I picked up the last piece of bacon and offered it to her. Lemon snatched it out of my fingers and devoured it in one swift burnt crunch before lolloping off after Hope.

I sat for a moment after they'd gone, trying to figure out how Joe Marcus had frightened the girl so badly and why.

Had she seen what happened to Kyle Stephens, I wondered, or had they simply threatened her with the same fate?

Ten

RILEY FLEW US IN LOW over the city. Hope, Lemon and I, along with a dig team made up of Thai, Japanese, Brit and US members, and another shrink-wrapped pallet of emergency supplies bound for who-knows-where. We squeezed around it inside the cargo bay, which didn't make for easy conversation. Neither did it make for comfort.

Some time during the night Riley had managed to beg, steal, or borrow a replacement winch for the Bell and refitted it. It may even have been the same one he'd accused the local police of filching for their own aircraft but I didn't ask and he wasn't saying.

It was bright enough that I could slip on a pair of sunglasses and stare without being obvious about it. If I thought I'd imagined him trying deliberately to dislodge me when I'd leapt for the helicopter the previous day, that period of observation confirmed my fears. His flying was flawless but his expression betrayed a conflicted man. At least it would seem he hadn't been *happy* about trying to kill me.

Well, that was always comforting to know.

But the question remained—why? Was it his own idea or was Joe Marcus pulling everyone's strings behind the scenes?

Riley was as relaxed about aviation inflight rules as he was about everything else, so we flew with the side door slid back, which at least created a swirling influx of cooler air inside the fuselage.

We made one stop along the way, to drop the dig team at their start-point location. They left with cheery goodbyes to Hope and pats to Lemon. I received the occasional nod—the new recruit who has yet to prove themselves in combat.

Lemon seemed perfectly happy to be up in a helicopter, if not actually blasé about it. She lay panting beneath Hope's canvas seat, wearing a harness with a fluorescent vest built in and bootees on all four feet. The bootees were clearly styled after human hiking boots. Bright colours, hi-tech shape, rugged soles, held in place with Velcro straps. It was rather unsettling to see a dog wearing them, doubly so when she lay down between us and stretched out her front legs.

Once we were under way Hope had recovered something of her balance. As if she was only really at ease when she was working.

Well, I can relate to that.

Now, she noticed my bemused glance at the dog's feet. "You never know what's going to be out there on the ground," she shouted over the rotor noise as though forgetting that we were both wearing headsets. "If Lem cuts her feet she could be out of action for weeks. She was a bit embarrassed about wearing 'em at first, but she's used to 'em now, aren't you, girl?"

She ran her hand over the dog's head. I could have sworn Lemon rolled her eyes again.

"Coming up on your search grid, ladies," Riley warned from the pilot's seat. "Please keep your arms and legs inside the car at all times and remain seated until the aircraft has come to a complete stop at the gate and the captain has switched off the Fasten Seatbelts sign."

Now it was Hope's turn to roll her eyes. "One of these days, Riley," she said, "you're going to do that routine and it will actually get the laugh you think it deserves."

He chuckled and managed not to cough. "Well I'm going to bloody well keep doing it until it does," he said. "Grab your gear."

Even though I'd checked through my pack before we left, I gave it another quick onceover, aware Hope was doing the same. We both carried food, water, a basic First Aid kit, GPS locator and two-way radios with a hands-free earpiece. Hope also had extra food and water for Lemon and two large cans of aerosol paint. I didn't ask what she planned on gang-tagging while she was out.

In my pack I also had four spare magazines for the SIG Sauer P229 in the small of my back beneath my shirt. Overkill maybe, but if the US Marines' motto is *Semper Fi*, meaning Always Faithful, then I preferred the Coast Guard's version—*Semper Paratus*, Always Ready. I made sure Hope didn't get a sight of the gun. No point in making her more uneasy.

Her final piece of equipment was a bedraggled-looking chew toy clipped to her belt. Every now and again I noticed Lemon giving the toy a longing glance and guessed that play time was her reward for making a successful find.

Hope had expected me to carry the extra gear and she was put out when I refused. I guessed from her slightly affronted surprise that my predecessor had done so without argument.

That told me a lot about Kyle Stephens, Gulf Wars veteran or no.

So I gave her the usual speech. She didn't like it much, but they never do.

"I'm not here to be your pack mule—you carry your own kit," I told her. "If I have to, I'll carry you *and* whatever of your stuff I can't leave behind, but let's just pray it doesn't come to that."

"What about Lem?"

I shook my head. "I can't protect both of you. Your job is to look after your dog and my job is to look after you," I said. "If anything happens, I'll get between you and the threat. If I tell you to get down, get down. Don't ask why, just do it. There won't be time to start a debate and I will not be kidding. But unless we're actually under fire don't drop flat—just crouch as low as you can and be ready to move. If Lemon's out of sight and you tell her to stay put, will she do it?"

She seemed almost offended. "'Course. I trained her myself since she was a puppy."

"Well that's what you should do then. And if I tell you to run, you run like hell and find a place to hide until I shout for you. That's when you'll know it's safe."

"I don't care about me," Hope said, "but sometimes, if people are desperate to find someone, well, they think if they get hold of Lemon they can, I dunno, jump the queue, bypass the system. So—," her eyes skated over me, dubious now, even a little scared, "—how will I know they're not forcing you to shout out?"

I met her eyes. "They won't force me."

"But supposing..."

"I didn't say they wouldn't try," I agreed, "only that they won't succeed. I will not lure you into a trap, Hope. You can trust me on that."

She did not look convinced.

After Riley dropped us off at our designated point he was airborne again without hanging around. Anyone would think he expected incoming fire. I was reminded of the mad Israeli C-130 pilot, Ari.

Maybe they were all a little touched.

Maybe they had to be.

As Riley lifted off, with the Bell's rotor wash like a physical force pressing down on us and blasting dust into our faces, I heard his voice in my ear.

"Comms check, ladies."

"Five by five," Hope said.

I went for the slightly more conventional: "Loud and clear."

"Roger that. Be careful out there. And good hunting."

Eleven

"**S**EEK ON!"

Hope's instruction to Lemon was always the same, and every time the dog responded in the same way, bounding forwards with the kind of enthusiasm only Labrador retrievers really have nailed. She soon settled into an apparently meandering search pattern, leading with her nose.

I stayed a little way back and let the pair get on with it unhindered. The teamwork between the two of them, the sense of total trust, was fascinating to watch.

Every now and again Lemon would pause to stare back at her handler as if making sure of her approval. Hope never missed these glances and was always ready to urge her on. That they needed each other was obvious, as was the fact that neither of them wanted it any other way.

We were on what might once have been a fancy shopping street lined by old-fashioned buildings that had not stood up well to a quake of such magnitude. Many of the buildings had not stood at all. Of the ones that *were* still upright, it looked as though when the first tremors hit most of the revamped façades had simply sloughed away from the brickwork behind. Each had come crashing down like a concrete portcullis, crushing whatever happened to be below at the time.

I looked at the devastation and wondered how anybody, caught in such a location, could possibly have survived.

And if by some miracle they had, how the hell we were going to get them out without serious construction equipment and lifting gear, or possibly use of a Sikorsky S-64 SkyCrane.

In many ways the violently disturbed landscape reminded me of the Balkans immediately after the civil war. Constant bombardment reduced many of the once-beautiful cities to ruins such as this. Only the blast damage and the individual bullet holes and craters were missing.

That feeling of familiar unease put me on edge. It was totally against everything I'd ever learned, to be standing out in the open rather than using the jagged structures for cover and concealment. It felt even more wrong to allow my principal, Hope, to skyline herself on top of a mound of rubble as well.

Keeping her position always in the back of my mind, I scanned the wasteland as if expecting to catch the sight-flare of an enemy sniper. Everywhere I looked I saw the same indications of panic and sadness that always came with sudden attack regardless whether its origin was natural or man-made:

A single shoe, abandoned jewellery, a broken toy or a spilled shopping bag containing some kind pastry treats now gone bad and swarming with insects.

Lemon picked her way delicately over all this in her hi-tech bootees and squeezed between the twisted metal of cars that had once been parked nose-in toward the kerb. They were now squashed to the height of their wheels by the fallen masonry. She started at one end of the parade of boutique stores, disappearing in and out of tiny gaps without a qualm. Whenever she emerged she'd shake herself vigorously from nose to tail as if to get the dust out of her fur and look to Hope.

"Good girl, Lem. Good girl. No problem," Hope would tell her. "Seek on. That's my girl. Seek on."

And Lemon would trot off hunting for the next hidey hole to slip through.

The only other sound was Hope shaking the rattle cans of paint. Every time the dog left one of the buildings without indicating, Hope sprayed a prominent red square onto it, with the number 441 inside it. I was curious, but not so curious I wanted to disturb them long enough to ask about it.

Then, halfway down the west side of the street, Lemon came out of a building and immediately sat down, her expression anxious. Hope's hand shaking the paint can faltered. If it hadn't been for that, I might have thought the dog was simply tired. Hope looked hard at the building for a moment and then wordlessly replaced the red can in her bag and picked out the yellow instead.

She sprayed the same square with the same 441 inside, put the can away and took the chew toy off her belt.

Lemon leapt to her feet and lunged for the toy. Hope whisked it out of her way and launched it in a looping overhand throw. Lemon scrabbled for grip and galloped in pursuit, scudding up spurts of grit and small stones.

I moved up alongside Hope. She glanced at me and read the question I didn't need to ask.

"Body in there," she said briefly, jerking her head back towards the building. "When we've cleared somewhere it gets marked in red. Yellow means there's someone inside needs to be brought out. That way, when they're done the recovery team can overspray the yellow with red and there's no confusion."

Her voice was flat. It struck me again how young she looked to be working amid all this death, how she and the dog needed each other for emotional support as much as anything else.

I looked at the building again. There was no signage left on the front of it to show what kind of a store might have been in business there. Through gaps in the fallen masonry I surmised that the adjoining one, which we'd just cleared, had once sold clothing. I could see dismembered manikins still wearing the remnants of high-fashion labels with price tags to match. Now they were strewn like rags amid a glittering sea of broken glass.

Lemon reappeared with the chew toy in her mouth, head held high so it didn't snag on the debris at her feet. She looked inordinately proud of herself for this act of retrieval, delivering her spittle-covered gift into Hope's hands and grinning over it with her tongue lolling sideways. Hope dug out water and a treat from her pack. Lemon snatched the treat down in one gulp. I was reminded of my disappearing bacon.

"She's very polite," I said as Hope made a big fuss of her. "Most dogs I've come across make you work for it or just toss the thing at your feet."

"I taught her she always has to hand it over," Hope said, nodding to the glass that crunched beneath us. "Don't want her eating none of that."

I looked down and this time saw not only glass but something else sparkling amid the shards. Clear stones with far too regular a shape, ones that had been cut to show off their brightness and brilliance. And having seen one, I suddenly saw others. The significance of the colours slowly dawned on me. Not simply green, blue and red glass, but emeralds, sapphires and rubies.

Well, that answered the question of what kind of store it had been I supposed. It also supplied one of the reasons R&R needed a security presence. The prospect of bumping into looters out here was a very real one.

I nodded to the yellow spray, the corners beginning to dribble where the paint had gone on too thick. "What's with the four-four-one?"

"International phone code for the UK, which is forty-four, plus Lem and I are Team One." Again that hint of pride. "Joe says it's the easiest way to let the other teams know who marked it, so they can keep track. The Japanese crew tags with eighty-one, the New Zealanders sixty-four. That's pretty standard, I think. It was Joe came up with the colour scheme though."

"It's a good system," I agreed. The former Marine, it seemed, had a practical mind-set when it came to dealing with death.

But then, I'd already worked that one out.

"He's the best at what he does," Hope said as if reading my thoughts. Her face turned a little wistful. "That's why I wanted to work with him."

"How long have you been doing this kind of stuff?"

"Long enough." It had been a casual question but she stiffened as if I'd implied she had no experience on which to base her claim.

"I wasn't casting aspersions," I said mildly. "You have to admit, though, you don't look old enough to drive."

"I'm twenty," she said quickly. "That's old enough, isn't it?" She busied herself with packing away the dog's water bowl and clipping the chew toy back onto her belt. Lemon watched her with that slightly anxious expression back on her face.

Me and my mouth.

"Look, I'm sorry—" I began.

"'S OK. I 'spose I just get that a lot," she mumbled. "Hey, we really need to get back to work. Come on, Lem, you ready? Seek on then, girl. Seek on!"

Lemon bounced away again, sniffed a circle in front of the next storefront and limbo'd through another impossible gap.

As we moved off I glanced down but Hope was tidy and methodical. There was nothing left behind except the glittering shards of broken glass with the brighter sparks of diamonds among them.

But maybe—just maybe—I couldn't see quite as many as there were before. I would have asked her about that, but with perfect timing, Lemon chose that moment to reappear.

She shoved her head through and then wriggled her tight-packed body out of the narrow gap. She stood alert and quivering, her gaze totally focused on Hope, and let out half a dozen rapid barks.

Hope went rigid. Despite the heat of the day, all the hairs came up along my forearms.

"A live find," she mumbled for my benefit, although I hardly needed to be told. "Means she's made a live find."

I glanced over, saw the pallor of her thin features, the tension in her body.

"What colour do we spray for that?" I asked but she shook her head.

"We don't," she said, reaching for her radio. "We wait."

Twelve

THE DIG TEAM turned up half an hour later, by which time we'd already checked the remaining stores on that side of the street.

Lemon had shown little interest until she stopped abruptly and sat down again when she neared the end of the row. I was the one who ventured close enough to discover a family of three dead inside their flattened car. The child in the back was still strapped into his booster seat.

Hope made sure she threw Lemon's chew toy in the opposite direction, as if she didn't want the dog to see what it was she'd found. Maybe that was simply my take on things and it was Hope herself who didn't want to see.

All in all, it did not feel like a good time to ask about the gems lying in the street.

The dig team was a mix of nationalities led by a redheaded figure I instantly recognised despite his borrowed local police coveralls.

"Well, well, Charlie," Wilson said. "We meet again."

I shook the Glaswegian copper's hand. "Couldn't stay away, huh?"

He grinned at me, but when his eyes shifted across to Hope I saw his eyebrows lift a notch.

It was hard not to see what he saw—an impossibly young-looking girl and a Labrador who wasn't helping matters by acting like a brainless family pet on a run in the park.

"How are you liking the work with R&R then?" he asked.

"Early days yet."

"Well, let me know if you get fed up, eh?"

"Hang on. I thought you were after a job with Parker?"

He grinned. "Just keeping my options open. I hear it's quite a cushy number."

I thought of the near miss jumping for the Bell and gave him a wry smile. "It has its moments."

"Right then, we better get started," he said. "Want to show us the spot?"

Hope led him there with Lemon ambling beside her, the chew toy still clutched in her mouth and those remarkable green eyes unblinking. By the time they reached the place where Lemon had indicated, he was frowning.

"You're quite sure, eh?"

Hope flushed and put a defensive hand on the dog's head. "'Course," she said.

He glanced at me as if hoping to glean some information about how seriously to take this. "Joe Marcus tells me she's the best he's seen in a long time," I said without inflection.

Wilson considered this and then nodded. "Good enough."

"Isn't he coming—Joe, I mean?" Hope demanded.

"Not for this one," Wilson said. "Don't worry yourself though. I like my own skin too much to risk losing it needlessly. I've had a bit of experience myself, so we'll be careful, eh?"

Once the dig team got started it seemed clear to me that they knew what they were doing. They scanned with a portable gas leak detector before the two-stroke masonry saw came out. The fourteen-inch circular blade soon created a gap large enough for a man to crawl through.

The smallest of the diggers—a Japanese guy—was selected to go in. He wore a miner's hard hat with an LED lamp, as well as a safety harness with rope attached. They paid out the rope as he ventured further inside just as if he'd been caving. In a way I suppose he was.

Hope waited off to one side with Lemon. The girl's tension had communicated itself to the dog and the chew toy was failing to distract either of them. Lemon was snuffling around in the dirt and picking up small pebbles in her soft mouth which she solemnly offered to Hope. Hope took each one, ignoring the coating of slobber and put it absently into her pocket as if she didn't want to offend the dog by throwing away the gift. Her eyes were glued to the dig team as she wiped her hand down the side of her trousers.

Eventually the rope went slack and they began slowly to reel it in. The Japanese guy emerged with a mixture of concrete and brick dust smeared into the sweat on his face.

"I found a couple near the front wall of the main structure about ten yards back thataway. Man and a woman," he called across in a strong California accent. He looked at Hope. "I'd guess they've been dead a while. I'm sorry."

Wilson's gaze passed over me with a faint trace of scepticism before it landed on Hope. "Sorry, pal," he said. "Luck of the game, I guess."

"But...that can't be right." She stumbled over the words. "Lem told me...there's no *way* she's wrong..."

Wilson shrugged. "Well, we tried, eh?"

Hope's colour rose and fell fast as a traffic light. She moved nearer, put out a staying hand to the Japanese guy who'd just crawled from under the rubble. "You *have* to go again," she pleaded. "Lemon don't get it wrong. Once she's had a sniff of something she can follow it anywhere. You have to...please."

The Japanese guy hesitated and looked to his team leader, alarmed not so much by her vehemence as the possibility she was about to burst into tears.

"Hey, now," Wilson said. He went to put a placatory hand on Hope's arm but she jerked away from him. The habitual goofy smile on Lemon's face disintegrated into a snarling growl as she jumped stiff-legged between them.

Before I could intervene, Wilson jerked back instantly. He'd clearly encountered enough guard dogs in his time, both police and military, to be leery of them. Hope spun away with a wordless click of her fingers. Lemon followed as if attached to her leg by a very short chain, staring up at her handler and letting out a series of small high-pitched squeaks.

I came up alongside Wilson and watched her rigid stance with concern.

"Now what the feck was *that* all about, eh?" he asked softly.

I had my suspicions but I wasn't going to voice them. That would have raised too many questions, least of all about how I'd come by my knowledge. I shook my head.

"Supposing she *is* right? Do you want that on your conscience?" I waited a beat. "Do me a favour will you? You're here now. Just get your guy to take one more look."

The Japanese guy who'd discovered the woman's body was hovering, helmet in hand and the straps loosened on his harness. His eyes flicked between us, wary of the atmosphere. "I don't mind going again, dude. Better to be sure, huh?"

Wilson looked from one of us to the other and sighed. "How tight is it for space in there?"

The Japanese guy shrugged. "Once you get past the cars it opens out a little onto what used to be the sidewalk," he said. "We might need some help finding a way into the store itself, if we need to go that far."

Wilson nodded. "I better come with you then, pal," he said. "Give you a hand."

The Japanese guy pulled his harness tight again quickly, as if worried either of them might change his mind.

We watched in silence as the two men adjusted their hard hats and knee pads. Wilson folded several body bags into his coveralls, knowing he'd need a couple and, I supposed, hoping he wouldn't need more.

Then they crawled carefully back through the gap they'd created. Even Hope edged closer again while Lemon plonked herself down in the dust and twisted round to nip at an itch on her back. Flies buzzed around our heads, their drone mixing with the distant chop of rescue, police and military helicopters.

Two of the dig team held the men's safety lines, letting them out steadily through their gloved fingers as the pair worked their way deeper inside. It struck me then that they weren't actually safety lines at all—they were recovery lines, should the worst happen.

And just as that cheery thought formed in my head, the ground began to tremble under our feet.

Thirteen

SOMEBODY SHOUTED, "Aftershock!" and there
was a concerted rush away from what was left of the nearest
buildings while we could still stand.

The tremble became a shudder that grew in violence
until it was like being back in the Hercules dropping
through holes in the sky. I'd never experienced the feel of
severe turbulence while still at ground level before. I half
dropped to my knees before I was thrown the rest of the
way. Around me the others flattened themselves too, an
instinctive reaction.

I lifted my head briefly to check on Hope's position. She
was well out in the open, crouched on knees and elbows as
the training dictated. She had one hand wrapped round the
back of her neck and the other latched through the dog's
collar. Lemon lay on her belly alongside, crowding in with
her ears flat, trying to lick Hope's face. I wasn't sure if she
was offering comfort by doing this, or taking it.

The rumbling through the ground was like the biggest heaviest subway train passing directly beneath us. It must have had a load of carriages, too, because it went on and on for more than twenty seconds before it finally began to die away.

I had to remind myself there *was* no subway and no train.

Staggering to my feet, I struggled to get my balance now the earth was still.

"Everybody OK?" I called. I got a series of cautious nods and waves by way of reply. I moved quickly over to where the safety lines snaked out from between the cars. To do so I had to hop across a crack in the road that I was damn sure hadn't been there a few minutes previously. Wisps of dust or steam rose gently from it like an outward breath.

"Wilson!" I shouted, ashamed that I didn't know the other guy's name. I listened a moment. Nothing. I turned to nearest member of the dig team. "Let's get them out of there. Do they have their radios?"

A handset was shoved at me. It was the same as mine, just tuned to a different frequency. I pressed the transmit button.

"Wilson, this is Fox. You guys OK in there?"

I half-expected an eerie silence but instead the Scot's laconic tones came back to me right away.

"Aye, but I'd appreciate you not stamping around out there in the big boots, pal," he said, coughing. "That last one brought down a mite of debris, but we're clear and Ken thinks we may have a way through, so looks like it's done us a favour, eh? We'll bag up the two dead and hook up our lines so you can pull them out—give us more room to work with. Three birds, one stone, eh?" He began coughing again.

"Have that," I said. "Standing by."

We waited until there was a jerk on his recovery line and then dig team began the slow and solemn process of hauling the first corpse out of the rubble.

Wilson and the Japanese guy, Ken, appeared briefly at gap between the cars to help push the body bag the last

few feet. Their clothing and faces were caked in dust. I unclipped Wilson's line and passed it back to him.

They repeated the process with the second body, which was larger and took more effort. We were all sweating in the heat by the time we were done. Wilson took off his helmet briefly to wipe his face.

"All right, we'll go take another look for this live one. Standard radio checks every five minutes," he said to one of his team. He put a hand on the body bag we'd just pulled clear. "Let's hope we don't need another of these, eh?" And with that he disappeared back into the void.

Between us we carried the bodies of the dead couple clear and laid them down gently. Two labels were written in clear characters, assigning each of them a Unique Reference Number that would stay with them until they were finally identified and reconciled.

The rest of the dig team had been working to retrieve the family in the crushed car. There were already another couple of body bags laid out on the open ground and we put our burden alongside it, also with URN labels attached.

From the size of one of the bags, I judged that was the child from the back seat. A member of the dig team crossed himself, lips moving in some silent prayer.

I turned away, just in time to see a new group approaching, picking their way along the half-blocked road. Something about the way they moved had me reaching a hand for the SIG at my back, but then I stilled. The coveralls they wore were the same as the police officers I'd seen waiting to pick up Wilson at the airport. Even the moustaches and the aviator sunglasses looked the same, too. They were all armed. Old-fashioned leather holsters with a press-stud flap, making it impossible to gauge what lay inside.

Again I checked on Hope's location, made sure she was well back, and then waited for them to reach us, calling a casual hello before they got too close.

They stopped, as I'd hoped they would, before they were among us. One man pushed forward, giving a desultory wave.

"The aftershock came just after we landed," he said, indicating some unseen helo off behind his group, hidden by the tumbled buildings. "We're just checking everyone here is OK, yes?"

He was middle-aged and slim apart from a protruding belly, but he was coping well with the heat and didn't look out of breath having to pick his way over rough terrain.

"We're fine," I said, noting the way his eyes slid to the body bags and the team members crouched by the gap between the cars with the two recovery lines stretching inside. "I didn't know anyone else was working this sector."

He regarded me for a moment, his eyes impossible to read behind the aviators. "I'm Peck," he said at last, motioning to the police insignia on the breast pocket of his coveralls. "Divisional commander."

His official ID was on a lanyard around his neck, with the plastic badge tucked out of the way into the pocket. I wore my own the same way and now I lifted it clear between two fingers.

"Charlie Fox, R&R," I said, adding pleasantly, holding it level for him to read. "And now you've seen mine I'm sure you won't object to showing me yours?"

Clearly he *did* object but there wasn't much he could do to refuse. He freed his ID and would have flashed it briefly but I managed to snag it for a closer look. I matched the picture to the man in front of me and surreptitiously checked the laminated edges for tampering.

"Thanks. Sorry about that," I said with a shrug as I handed it back. *Only following orders, guv.* "But I'm under strict instructions from Joe Marcus to verify everyone."

Marcus hadn't mentioned anything of the sort, but the name had resonance for Peck, I could tell, even though he tried to hide his reaction behind a noncommittal grunt.

"Of course," he added quickly. "It would be my advice to you also." He stepped around me and headed for the body bags. Now I'd confirmed he was there in an official capacity I didn't see how I could reasonably object. I settled for being annoying rather than outright obstructive and ambled alongside him instead. That seemed to work.

"Where did you find these people?" he asked.

I let one of Wilson's team fill him in as the final body from the car was laid with the others.

When Peck spoke again his words might have been casual but his tone allowed little room for discussion. He pointed to the line of zipped bags and said, "I'd like to take a look."

Fourteen

COMMANDER PECK pulled down the zip on the first bag, revealing the woman from the car. She'd been in the passenger seat and closest to the falling masonry. Peck zipped the bag up again quickly and moved to the next. I glanced at the faces of Wilson's people and saw from their horrified reactions that this was a long way from normal procedure.

To everyone's relief, I think, Peck passed over the child's figure and unzipped the second bag. The man who'd been driving had survived a little longer and at least had a face Peck could frown over.

I heard movement behind me. Hope was scrambling towards us.

"Hey, what's he doing?" she demanded. "Leave them alone."

Peck barely glanced at her. "It is my duty to make immediate identifications if that is possible," he said. "This is my area and I have received many missing persons' reports. Some of these persons may well be known to me."

He took longer looking at the male corpse Wilson and Ken had dragged out, although I would hazard a guess that the man's own mother would not have recognised his face. Peck was thorough, patting all the pockets, but he found no ID, closed the bag again and bent over the woman.

"You shouldn't be doing that!" Hope protested, more loudly now. Her eyes shot to mine. "Charlie, can't you make him stop?"

"Commander," I snapped, "I'm sure you'll get your chance to make formal IDs once the bodies have been transported to the official mortuary."

But he'd already opened the body bag and was dipping his hands into the woman's pockets without taking any notice. When he straightened, he had a wallet in his hands which he flipped open.

"Hmm. This one I think I do know of. I will check with headquarters," he announced. "You will be informed." And he shut the wallet again before slipping it into the side pocket of his coveralls.

Hope moved forward and got in his face. Her eyes were barely on a level with the base of Peck's nose, but she suddenly seemed bigger. Maybe that had something to do with the fact that Lemon was standing beside her, growling deep in her chest. A line of fur had risen from the back of her neck and tapered away down her spine.

Peck was watching the dog very carefully. Lemon pulled back her lips and treated him to a display of every one of her impressive teeth. Without taking his eyes off her, his right hand slid up and meaningfully unsnapped the stud securing his holster.

By the time he'd done so the SIG was out in my hand and lined up on the bridge of his nose.

"Hey," I said quietly. "She—and the dog—are under my protection. Think carefully before you act."

Peck shifted his eyes from the end of the SIG's barrel to my face and beyond it. He showed his teeth in a similar way to Lemon and said then, "I would strongly advise you to do the same, my friend."

Behind me I heard the unmistakable metallic click of the hammer being thumbed back on a service pistol.

"Oh, I always think before I act," I said. "And either way it goes, the outcome for you does not look promising, does it?"

He absorbed that in glowering silence before signalling curtly to the man behind me. I heard the hammer released, the rasp of leather, and only then allowed my arm to drop.

Hope was staring at the pair of us, wild-eyed. Wilson's own dig team looked as though they were praying for another aftershock—one big enough to open up a massive sink-hole and swallow the lot of us.

The radio clipped to the shoulder of Peck's coveralls began to squawk then. He reached for it, adjusted one of the knobs and tilted it towards his mouth, pointedly turning his back on me. I used the opportunity to glance behind me and met the stony faces of his men. It was difficult to tell which of them had drawn on me. They all looked eager for the task.

Peck finished his transmission and rapped out orders. He turned back and gave us a nod. "I am needed elsewhere," he said.

I'm sure I wasn't the only one who resisted the urge to say, "Good."

His men had already begun to move off but before he could do so himself, Hope stepped forwards. Unaccountably, I saw she was offering him a shy smile.

"I'm sorry—about before," she said in a slightly breathy voice. "I didn't mean to be rude. And Lemon's just a bit over-protective of me, aren't you, girl?" She looked down to the dog who was staring back up at her adoringly. "She's just a big softy really." Hope seemed to give a little twitch that might have been a shrug.

Lemon skipped over to Peck and butted him in the knees in a clumsy display of affection. Reluctantly, he leaned down to pat her flank and, seemingly encouraged by this, she bounced up and got her booteed feet nearly to his shoulders. He staggered back under the unexpected weight with a sharp curse.

Hope gave a rather ineffectual cry of, "Lemon!" and dashed to grab the dog's collar, but struggled to drag her off him. Then she started frantically brushing the dirt and dust bootprints left by the dog's feet from his clothing. She wasn't too careful where she put her hands and after a moment he paddled her away, face flushing. And all the time, Lemon leapt around them, barking.

"Please!" Peck said stiffly. "Please, it is no matter. I am dressed for the work."

It was neatly done. The noise, the dancing dog, the profuse apologies and exaggerated waving of hands that acted as a complete distraction. So I was probably the only one who noticed Hope's nimble fingers slip into the police commander's coverall pocket. When they came out again the dead woman's wallet was pinched between them. But by the time the girl had pulled Lemon a few strides away and calmed her, her hands were empty and her face was without guile.

Into the quiet that followed came a burst of radio static. Not from Peck's police network this time, but from one of the handsets issued to the dig team. And then, loud and clear, I heard Wilson's voice over the air:

"Hey! We got someone here. We got someone. And he's still alive!"

Fifteen

I SAT IN A HOSPITAL CORRIDOR waiting to talk to a man who might or might not regain consciousness. Been there, done that. Didn't like it much the last time.

It was only mid-afternoon but already it had been a very long day that was barely halfway over.

The whole atmosphere had changed out there with the realisation of a live find. A sudden energy and purpose swept over everyone as they put their strategies into operation. There was nothing worse, I was told, than finding someone alive but bringing them out dead.

I could think of a few things that were infinitely worse, but I kept them to myself.

Commander Peck and his men slipped away before they could be volunteered to help dig. And as soon as they were out of sight Hope used the increased level of activity to cover her return of the wallet to the dead woman's body bag. Just for a second I debated on tackling her about that deft sleight of hand, but decided against. Her ability was curious, but until I knew if it was significant to the death of Kyle Stephens it was better to pretend I hadn't seen a thing.

That was the trouble with uncovering secrets—you couldn't pick and choose.

Getting the injured man out of the ground was a painstaking task that called for many different kinds of expertise. Keeping him alive until he could be freed, and not bringing down the rest of the building on top of him in the process were the two main difficulties. Wilson radioed in for reinforcements and it did not surprise me that the two figures next on scene were Joe Marcus and Dr Bertrand, arriving in the khaki-coloured Bell with Riley at the flight controls. He set down with a casual elegance onto the uneven piles of bricks at the end of the street.

Dr Bertrand swept past us and immediately started interrogating the dig team about the condition of the casualty. But Joe Marcus took a moment to have a word with Hope. She seemed bursting to tell him something, but he put a hand on her arm to stay her. Even from a distance I could see his lips form a single word: "Later."

As he turned away and caught me watching the pair of them, his gaze issued a flat challenge:

You may think you've just seen something but you haven't, and if you're wise you won't push this further.

What makes you think I'm wise?

But the most interesting thing about the encounter, to my mind, was the fact that when Joe Marcus touched her, Hope didn't flinch at all.

Lemon was sent in twice more, under Hope's direction, to pinpoint the position of the trapped man more accurately. I heard her barking in there as if to say, "It's so obvious. What's the matter with you people?"

I helped load the three bodies into the Bell. They had each been tagged with a Unique Reference Number, with the same URNs added to the bags of personal items collected from close nearby.

It was not the first time I'd handled body bags but I can't say I've ever enjoyed the experience, and it's not something you want to get used to. The bodies inside graunched and folded in places they were not supposed to fold when fully intact.

"I'll drop them off at the morgue after we've got this other guy to hospital," Riley said. But he glanced back frowning at the lumps of masonry that were being cleared away from the man's position. "Or maybe I'll only have to make the one stop, you reckon?"

But against all the odds, they brought the buried man out alive. He was bleeding from a vicious head-wound, crazed, dehydrated, barely conscious and with the bones of his left forearm visible for the world to see, but he appeared to have escaped the worst of what might have been.

Dr Bertrand pumped him full of painkillers via a rapidly inserted cannula into the back of his right hand, stabilised his left arm, put a neck collar on him and set up a bag of fluids. She moved with brisk efficiency and inside a couple of minutes he was on a stretcher being carried towards the Bell.

"Charlie, go with 'im and get 'is identity," Dr Bertrand ordered. "Oh, and see if the woman found nearby was known to 'im, also."

Maybe it was the lack of "please" or "thank you" that made me dig my heels in enough to argue. "My place is here, with Hope," I said. "I promised I wouldn't go anywhere without her."

The doctor had been already turning away and she stopped as if amazed to be questioned. It was Joe Marcus who stepped in.

"Hope's done enough for the day. She'll be heading back with us so there's nothing for you here," he said quietly, a host of meanings concealed beneath his measured tone. "But that guy will have family waiting for him. Going with him—maybe finding out his story—will put someone else's mind at rest."

Not much I could say to that, really, which was how I came to be sitting on an uncomfortable plastic chair in a hospital corridor at midnight, waiting.

He was in surgery for a fractured skull, I was told. They would let me know as soon as he was in recovery.

By chance I saw one of the same nurses who'd taken charge of the boy from the roadside the day before. I stopped her briefly as she hurried past and asked about him.

"I'm so sorry. He...didn't make it," she said. "We did everything we could but in the end we lost him." She frowned at me, weariness in her face, her voice and her body. "I called Dr Bertrand last night. Didn't she pass on the news?"

"No." I shook my head. The nurse seemed disturbed enough for me to add a harmless fiction: "I'm sure she meant to—when she had a moment."

The nurse nodded and dashed away.

I settled back in my chair. It seemed only yesterday that I had waited, on and off, for nearly four months in chairs like these. Waited for Sean Meyer to come back to me.

And he almost had.

Sixteen

EVEN THOUGH THE SEAN MEYER I got back was not the same man who left me behind in that split second between the finger pulling the trigger and the bullet leaving the gun, I still thought there might be a chance for us.

Right up until Mexico City.

Not that Sean went to Mexico City, and perhaps that omission was at the heart of the matter. His first time out in the field since his recovery had not ended well and he was vacillating about his whole future in the close-protection industry.

Parker refused to accept his resignation and instead persuaded him to take care of glad-handing clients at the office in New York while Parker himself went back to the sharp end of the game as needed.

For this reason, when a high profile assignment came up south of the border Sean stayed to co-ordinate things at home and I flew out there as part of a team that included Parker.

The Mexico City job had been hazardous but successful—one of those rare occasions when everything just goes right. It hadn't been without incident but, even when we came under fire, the plans, backup plans and contingencies we'd put in place all unfurled like a dream and the clients were left seriously singing our praises.

In the army they drummed into us that no battle plan ever survives first contact with the enemy. I suppose there has to be an exception that proves every rule.

We landed at La Guardia on the return journey and Parker drove us into the city. He was still on a post-combat high. I'd never seen my normally calm and contained boss so buzzed up but his enthusiasm was infectious.

It hadn't abated by the time he pulled up at the kerb outside my apartment building. Living closest to the office I was the last of the team to be dropped off, so it was just the two of us.

We sat there for a while in one of the company Navigators with the engine running quietly, still going over the details, trying to work out how something good could be made even better. Eventually—with reluctance, I admit—I climbed out to retrieve my bag from the back. When I slammed the Navigator's rear door and turned, I found Parker waiting for me on the kerb.

"Thanks again, Charlie," he said, a smile crinkling the corners of his eyes.

"What for?"

"For being a superstar," he said. "Money can't buy the kind of great publicity we'll score from this job."

He was grinning like a kid. On impulse, I stepped forward and gave him a hug.

Mistake.

Before I knew it he'd lifted and swung me round off my feet.

"Parker! You idiot, put me down."

He did so, still grinning, but I saw the moment his expression shifted, saw those cool grey eyes flick down to my mouth and felt his arms tighten around me.

"Parker—" I said again. A warning this time, but it was already too late.

His head dipped. His kiss was a taste, a delicate nip that became a headlong plunge. His hands came up to frame my face, thumbs smoothing the line of my jaw, the hollow under my cheekbone, fingers at the base of my skull.

At that moment it would have been so easy to let myself fall into him, weightless. All the pent-up frustration, the feeling of utter rejection, the longing, suddenly came flooding out of me as I began to tumble. Just for a second I kissed him back almost on a reflex. Then reality jolted in.

I brought my hands up to grasp his wrists but he had already broken the kiss. He wrapped his hands protectively around mine and touched our foreheads together, still holding me close.

"I know, I know, I'm sorry. I promised myself I wouldn't do this," he muttered. "But..."

His voice trailed away. I swallowed and found it took effort to speak.

"I'm sorry too," I said. "I should learn to keep my distance."

He gave a soft laugh. "Well, every now and again I'm glad you don't," he said. "If only it could be 'now'. *And* 'again'..."

I made a noise of protest in my throat and shifted my hands. He released me at once.

"I'll see you in the office tomorrow morning," he said, stepping back and striving for normal. He cleared his throat. "Debrief is at oh-nine-thirty."

"Yessir," I said, smiling. "Nine-thirty? You going soft on us, boss?"

He grinned as he turned away, making a 'don't go there' gesture with his hand, and threw back over his shoulder, "Get some rest, Charlie. You've earned it."

I was still smiling as I picked up my bag and slung the strap over my shoulder, watching the Navigator move out into traffic. I glanced up at the apartment block. I knew which windows belonged to the apartment Sean and I shared but there was no sign of life behind the glass.

I rode the lift up to our floor with the feel of Parker's mouth still on mine like an imprint. I scrubbed my hands across my face not caring if I smeared my makeup. I never wore much anyway and a very long, very hot shower was first order of business.

As I unlocked our front door and moved along the hallway I called out, but there was no reply. The place was silent and empty. I felt my shoulders droop and wondered if it was with disappointment or relief.

At the edge of the living area I let the bag strap slide off my shoulder, unzipped it and dug inside for my gun case. I'd cleaned and stripped the SIG for transport in secure hold baggage, and I would clean it again before I reassembled it in the morning. But right now the shower beckoned.

I shoved the weapon and my boxes of spare ammunition into the gun safe mounted in the floor of the main bedroom, taking a quick glance round while I was in there. Sean kept the place so orderly it bordered on impersonal. I wondered if it was an indication of his state of mind.

I abandoned my travel bag and headed straight for the bathroom, stripping off as I went and leaving my travel-stained clothing where it fell. Then I stood under needles of water dialled lethally hot with my eyes closed and my hands braced against the tiles.

I don't know how long I'd been in there but the glass walls of the shower cubicle were steamed opaque when Sean Meyer's voice cut through the drumming downpour.

"Trying to wash away the guilt along with the smell of him are you, Charlie?"

I twisted blindly in the direction of the sound, gasping into the humid air, but the combination of wet hair and water in my eyes meant I could hear but not see him. All I knew was he was somewhere close.

It seemed a long time since Sean had wanted to see me naked to the point where he'd deliberately invaded my space like this. We still shared the apartment but very much separately. We hadn't shared a bedroom—never mind a bed—for months. It never occurred to me to lock the bathroom door because he hadn't shown the least inclination to walk in on me.

After the shock of his arrival, it took longer for the words themselves to penetrate.

"Trying to wash away the guilt along with the smell of him..."

What the—?

Furious, I swiped a hand across the glass at head-height and glared out. Sean was leaning in the doorway still dressed for the office. As a nod to being off duty he'd discarded his tie and the jacket of his dark grey suit, and rolled back his shirtsleeves. With his arms folded across his chest the action showed off the muscle bulk he'd worked so hard to regain after the coma.

He couldn't have made me feel more trapped if he'd set his mind to it.

I prayed that was not the case.

"I didn't realise you were here," I said, struggling to keep my voice neutral, as if nothing unusual or unsettling was taking place. There was no way I wanted to start an argument from this kind of disadvantaged position. "I'll be out shortly. Can you give me a few minutes?"

Instead he levered away from the doorframe and stalked forwards, letting his arms drop. I resisted the urge to cover my body from his gaze. Even with all its wounds and scars, it was nothing he hadn't seen before.

But not like this.

Even so, I didn't expect him to yank open the cubicle door heedless of the pounding spray. The steam roiled out, sucking a billowing waft of cold air in over my skin which goose bumped instantly.

"Sean!" I protested, low and shaky. "Get out!"

But he just stood there, subjecting me to a long scrutiny while his hair and clothing absorbed the sodden heat.

I felt my chin lift, my shoulders square. I met his gaze with defiance despite the colour flaring in my cheeks.

"What I asked," he repeated with deadly precision, "was—"

"I know what you damn well asked," I threw back, not bothering to waste my breath on questions when it was only too obvious what he'd been asking. "But if you think I'm going to discuss that kind of wild accusation in here like this—"

"What better time?" he demanded. "And where better place?"

And before I knew it he'd swung the door wide and stepped fully dressed into the shower with me.

The water beat his hair flat to his skull and ran from his brows, pushing his eyes into shadow behind the flow. The shirt turned transparent in a moment, the dry-clean-only suit trousers ruined.

The shower cubicle was a generous size. We'd shared it in the past but back then we'd been more than happy to occupy the same footprint, the same heartbeat. Now, when I was trying to keep him from touching me, it seemed impossibly small.

Sean bunched me back into the tiled wall, grabbed both wrists and wrenched my hands above my head, holding them there bracketed in his left. He was right-handed, but the gunshot wound to his left temple had affected his right side and he was still building back the strength of his grip. The fact he'd deliberately chosen to use the hand currently stronger, going against natural dominance, sent alarm bells clanging inside my head.

"I wasn't 'here' when you arrived, but I was close by all right," he said then in a savage whisper. "Close enough to see your fond farewell to Parker. The man *you* work for. The man *I'm* in partnership with. The man I'm supposed to trust."

I jerked my hands but he tightened his grip, stretching my arms a little more taut overhead until my muscles began to quiver. He leaned in, right hand fisted into the wall alongside me for balance. And all the time the water lashed down on the pair of us like a tropical typhoon.

"So how long's it been going on between the two of you, Charlie? Were you using him as a substitute for me all those months when I wasn't around to...satisfy you? Just how long did you wait before you and he—"

"Enough!" I snapped, my voice vibrating with anger. "Think the worst of me if you want, Sean. Why not? You always did before. But leave Parker out of this!"

"How can I?" he demanded, "when I saw the way you went to him out there, and I saw the way he kissed you. Got it bad, hasn't he?" He leaned in closer still, so the water splashed from his face down onto mine. I told myself that was the reason I shut my eyes. "So I think I have a right to know—does he touch you like this?"

I began, "You have no rights—"

Sean's free hand slicked up my ribcage to cup my breast, tormenting with fingers that knew how to cause both intimate pleasure and pain. Too long denied, I responded in spite of myself. Heat blossomed low in my belly, flushing the surface of my skin.

Sean sensed it and gave a mirthless laugh.

"Or this?"

He claimed my mouth in punishment while his hands balanced me teetering between restraint and caress.

I gasped onto his tongue and he swallowed the little mewl as if stealing my voice and my soul. From the first,

Sean had seemed to know all my body's secrets. Hell, he had created most of them. I tore my mouth free.

"I've never slept with Parker!" I cried wildly. "Yes, I know how he feels about me. But he knows I can't give him what he truly wants and he would never force me to try."

I don't know what finally got to him. Maybe it was the word "force" that did it. That and the fact that Parker—his friend, even his mentor—would not stoop so low.

Sean's head lifted. I felt the shift in his balance, braced my right arm and jerked down hard with my left, rotating my fist against the joint between his forefinger and thumb— the weakest part of his grip. Pulled in opposite directions, his hand sprang open.

I let my knees sag until I was almost squatting in the shower tray, then drove my heels downwards and surged up again. I kept my arms bent close to my chest and used the power from my legs instead. Both clenched fists landed in the fleshy vee beneath Sean's ribs, angled sharply upwards, with enough force even in the confined space to paralyse his diaphragm.

He fell back, chest heaving as he tried to claw air into his lungs. Without bothering to shut off the water I looped my arm through his from the front and kept him going. Before he knew it I'd marched him backwards out of the shower cubicle, stumbling through the bathroom and into the hallway.

The punch was an improvised close-quarter technique that came from the necessity of fighting in an enclosed space. The arm lock was standard for neutralising and removing troublemakers from a crowd. I wondered if Sean would find it ironic that he was the one who'd taught it to me.

In the living area I manoeuvred him around my open travel bag and sent him sprawling over the arm of the sofa. He landed heavy on the cushions, still shuddering for breath and now shivering in his drenched clothes.

The suit was past repair in any case, so I wasn't careful how I stripped him of his trousers and everything beneath. Why should I be the only one naked?

He didn't help but I didn't need him to. About half the shirt buttons remained attached. The rest were scattered to the four corners.

At least his Breitling wristwatch was waterproof to greater depths than we'd just plumbed. I was unfastening the strap by the time he had the breath to speak.

"Charlie," he rasped. "What the hell are you doing?"

He tried to bat my hands away but he was still in enough respiratory distress to make it a poor attempt. I twisted his wrist into another lock, one I could maintain using only two fingers and my thumb. With my free hand I reached for him, let him feel my nails curve against the most sensitive area of his skin.

He froze. I could almost see the beads of sweat pop out among the water on his forehead.

"What am *I* doing?" I echoed tightly. "What do you bloody well think? I'm doing the same to you as you were going to do to me."

I watched his eyes as I said it and watched the flare in them, the way his pupils dilated. It might be lust rather than love, but I told myself at this stage I'd settle for what I could get.

I tightened my grip, relentless. He might have forgotten the last four years we had together but I had not. Every place I'd ever touched him, every time I'd sent him up in flames for me, I could recall in clear and utter detail.

And now I used that knowledge coldly, ruthlessly, to drive any jealous thoughts of Parker, disdain for me or disgust with himself, right out of his head. By the time I released the lock on his wrist he could do nothing but hold onto me.

But in the morning, he was gone.

Seventeen

"**A**LL I COULD THINK ABOUT was getting out of there."

The man in the hospital bed had his eyes fixed on mine but I knew he didn't see me. His voice was raspy from the screaming and the acid-etch of concrete dust in his throat.

"How much can you remember?" I asked, but he let his head drop and I realised I should have reworded the question. *How much are you willing to remember?*

"I mean, it would help if we could start with who you are?" I said, trying to give out an encouraging vibe, "You weren't carrying any identification when you were found."

He frowned for a moment and then said, "My name is Santiago Rojas. I came here from São Paulo in Brazil, I think ten years ago. This much I know. I remember my past, my family back home, my work there, but here?" He gave me a hesitant smile and gestured toward his head. "I am struggling to recall anything about the last few years, never mind last week, or yesterday."

"Don't try to force it. It will come back to you in its own time," I said but I looked at the dressings around the surgical repairs to his skull and could not prevent the voice in the back of my mind from adding, *if it's going to come back at all...*

He nodded and used his unbroken arm to push himself uneasily straighter against the thin hospital pillow. There was only one to cushion him against the angled metal bedframe, but the way the casualties had been coming in steadily from all over the city, he was lucky even to have a bed.

"Can you perhaps tell me," Rojas asked, "was I found at my place of work? I know I have a store in the tourist district—I sell jewellery and deal in precious stones."

His voice carried a hint of something, as if he was trying to remind himself as much as inform me. And suddenly it was fiercely important to me that he *did* remember. For those close to him, if not for himself.

Don't project, I told myself. *It's not the same.*

Something about Rojas told me he would have been a good salesman of jewellery. Standard-issue hospital gowns are a great social leveller but he had well-looked after skin and expressive eyes. The fingernails that weren't torn were well manicured and polished smooth.

And more than that, he was aware of what he did with his hands, even the one in the cast. Each little gesture was imbibed with forethought and meaning, maybe even that certain sensuality that women seem to require when buying precious gems. I'd watched enough of them do so to have formed a theory. It was as if they needed to feel precious themselves, to feel worthy. Rojas's manner, his eyes and his hands, would have given that to them.

I explained what had happened to the street of boutique stores where he had his business, about the stone façades and the devastation. I didn't set out to give him nightmares by describing exactly *how* he'd been buried after the collapse of the storefronts, but when he pressed me I wasn't going to lie to him.

Rojas looked down at his hands as if amazed to find them still attached to his body.

"Holy Mother of God," he said, genuine awe in his voice. "I asked the wrong question. It should not have been 'where' did you find me, but 'how'?"

"For that you have to thank a very talented search and rescue dog called Lemon," I said. "And Hope, who is Lemon's very persistent handler. She's the one who made them keep looking for you."

"Hope," he repeated softly. "What a beautiful name for a woman with such dedication."

For a moment I thought he'd got the wrong person. It seemed a strange description of the skinny girl with the quick fingers and the dog who was, it seemed, trained for far more than just searching.

"She's a constant source of wonder," I agreed.

"It is *my* hope," he said with a smile, "that I am able to meet with her? To express my thanks."

"I'm sure she'll appreciate that, although it was a team effort." And I told him about Wilson and California Ken, who were both volunteers from police forces on different sides of the world. I told him about Joe Marcus keeping him safe, about Dr Bertrand keeping him alive, and Riley airlifting him to hospital to ensure he had the best chance of remaining so. But that meeting any of them in person might be tricky. "There is still a lot to do out there—still a lot of missing people to be found."

He looked momentarily shocked. "I would not expect her to interrupt her work, of course," he said quickly. "Perhaps there is some small way I can repay her...?"

He let his voice trail off suggestively. I gave him a bland stare. "Hope works for an organisation called Rescue &

Recovery International," I said. "They are supported by grants and donations. I'm sure they'd welcome any amount you'd care to give them, however modest."

In fact, I'd no idea what R&R's policy was on people who wanted to pay them for their efforts, but I hardly thought they'd be turning money away.

Not if the rumours were correct...

I thought of Mrs Hamilton's concerns about R&R, and remembered again the way Hope's nimble fingers had dipped into the police commander's pocket so smoothly he never felt a thing. But I also remembered the way she'd put the wallet back among the dead woman's possessions, all without knowing I'd clocked what she was doing.

How did that square with the rumours?

"Do you know if I was alone?" Rojas asked now, a little diffident. He gestured to his head. "I do not even know if I have staff who work for me, or if they were working yesterday."

It was two days ago now, but I didn't think I ought to tell him that. One of many things I didn't ought to tell him, no doubt.

I hesitated. "If there was anyone else alive in the store with you when the earthquake hit," I said, "then it seems they didn't survive. They sent in the dog again after you were brought out and she didn't indicate anyone else. I'm sorry."

"But if they were dead, perhaps, and hidden from—"

"Lemon can tell the difference," I said. "Trust me. I've watched her work. She found you even though there was a couple who were buried very close by who did not survive."

He frowned. "A couple...?" he repeated slowly. "A couple. Yes! I remember a couple. They came in to buy an engagement ring. A beautiful three-carat marquise-cut ruby. It had, I think, pave set diamonds in a rose and white gold setting. She was so happy—"

He cut off abruptly and blinked at me. "How is it that I can remember some things so clearly and not others?"

Rojas shifted his position again, lips thinned against the pain. They had realigned and plastered the compound fractures of his arm so that only the tips of his fingers protruded from the cast, yellow with iodine. He was still getting used to the weight of it and he moved awkward and slow.

"You've suffered a serious head injury," I said. "It's bound to have affected you more than you realise."

"You mentioned the couple who were found nearby. Did she...?" He looked on the verge of weeping. "Was the lady wearing a ring as I describe? If so, I may be able to help you identify her."

I had a brief recall of the way the body bag behaved when we had loaded it into the Bell. I had no idea what state the woman's face might have been in.

"It's possible you may not be able to visually identify her," I warned.

"Ah. Then I could at least identify the ring perhaps?" he said. "If I can help, I want to do so."

"I'll ask," I said.

He met my gaze with very dark liquid eyes and smiled. "Thank you," he said. "It feels important that I do this. I *need* to know."

A harried nurse appeared in the doorway and told me my time was up.

"If you have more questions, you will have to come back tomorrow," she said, "when he has rested."

I rose, pushed my chair to the side of the room.

"Is there anyone you would like me to contact for you, Mr Rojas?" I asked, looking back as I reached the doorway. "Your wife or family?"

"I am not married," he said automatically and then gave a quick smile. "At least, I do not believe so." His expression became stricken. "Do you think it is possible that I might have forgotten a wife? Children even?"

I thought of Sean, of what he'd remembered—and what he'd forgotten.

"Yes," I said gently. "I'm afraid that *is* possible."

Eighteen

I CALCULATED THE TIME DIFFERENCE and called Parker Armstrong back in New York.

It was late afternoon there. The weather before I left had been edging into a late autumn, the leaves falling in copper swathes to coat the grassy expanse of Central Park. The weather swung between being not quite cold enough for winter coats, but too chilled for summer wear. The streets and subway trains were filled with people who sweated or shivered accordingly.

Here it was hot with a humid overtone that made the day seem sullen. I stood by an open window while I made my call, but all that seemed to do was blow hot air into my face.

"Charlie!" Parker greeted me, as if hearing from me was the highlight of his day. I sincerely hoped that was not the case. "How's it going?"

"Fine." I paused. "Any word?"

"From Sean? No, I'm sorry," he said, at once more subdued. "Is that why you…?"

"No," I said. "I need you to check something out for me. Or I should say some*one*."

"OK. Shoot."

"There's a young girl here as part of the R&R team. A Brit—Hope Tyler—she's a dog handler. Search, rescue and recovery."

"Rescue *and* recovery?" Parker queried. "Unusual. In my experience they typically have specialised teams for search and rescue and then bring in the cadaver dogs when they're pretty sure there's nobody left to rescue."

I shrugged. "Well, Lemon seems to do just about everything bar tap dance and make the tea. And come to think of it I wouldn't put either of those things past her."

"Lemon?"

"Hope's dog. A rather beautiful yellow Labrador retriever."

"I have a great deal of respect for working dogs of any kind," Parker said with the fervour of an ex-military man himself. "But you think this Hope—and Lemon—may be involved in what happened to Stephens?"

"Possibly not," I said. "But like I said, she's young—and she's scared of something. She went very cagey as soon as I brought up Stephens' name."

"When you say 'young', how young?"

"Twenty apparently, but she seems a very young twenty," I said. "I don't ever remember being that young."

At Hope's age I'd been in and out of the army, lived through humiliation and disgrace and was halfway out the other side. I'd been beaten down to my knees and refused to be beaten further.

"So you don't have her tagged as a potential suspect?"

"I wouldn't rule out anything at this stage, but if she *is* caught up in this I'd say she was labour rather than management."

"Oh?"

There was a wealth of quick understanding in the single-word question. Another of the reasons I enjoyed working with Parker so much.

"The rumours Mrs Hamilton heard related to thefts," I said. "And whatever else Hope may be, from what I saw of her today she's also a very talented fingersmith."

"A what?"

"A pickpocket. She liberated a wallet from the local police commander in front of all his men and none of them saw a thing, although she had the dog deliberately running interference, which helped. They're quite a team—in more ways than the expected."

"If she's stealing from the cops, that kinda confirms the rumours, don't you think?"

"Hmm," I said, still undecided. "The wallet she liberated wasn't the good commander's to start with, and she took it in order to put it back where it belonged. Not the behaviour of your average thief."

"Sounds intriguing. I'll have Bill do some deep background and I'll get back to you soon as I can."

"There's one more thing about her," I said and hesitated. "It's only an impression and I could be wrong but—"

"I trust your instincts, Charlie," Parker said. "So should you."

"Thank you," I said. I took in a long warm lungful of air, let it curl out again. "She shows signs of having been through some kind of sexual assault. Could be in her distant past for all I know, but it still resonates. As soon as a male stranger gets too close she locks up and Lemon goes crazy."

Parker, to his credit, didn't ask if I was sure, but his tone was grave. "OK Charlie, leave it with me. I'll see that Bill makes it a priority to find out what we can about this girl."

"I suspect she might have been through the system," I said. "After all, she didn't acquire those sleight-of-hand

skills overnight. Not without a few false starts that probably got her nicked for it once or twice. She said she had to
work hard to persuade Joe Marcus to take her on. Wonder
what kind of a job interview *that* was."

"Good call. Anyone catch your eye apart from Hope?"

I gave a short laugh. "She's about the only one of them
who *isn't* capable of murder, to my mind, although the
way Lemon reacted earlier when she thought the girl was
under threat makes me wonder if Hope needs to be capable
herself. I wouldn't put anything past the others, though. I
suspect they've already had one pretty good go at getting
shut of me."

I heard Parker's indrawn breath, his muttered, "Let's
hear it, Charlie."

So I told him all about the rescue on the fallen section
of roadway, the precise jink of the Bell at exactly the right
moment to throw me off balance, and how close I'd been to
falling. And the reactions of Dr Bertrand and Joe Marcus
afterwards.

"I guess if I said I wanted you on the next flight out it
wouldn't do me any good, would it?" Parker asked. "Your
job is to protect them from threat, not become a human
target."

"But that's exactly what I agreed to," I pointed out.
"And in fact it was what *you* promised Mrs Hamilton I was
more than capable of doing. Don't make liars of both of us,
Parker."

The long moment's silence at the other end of the
phone line was not solely due to the signal bouncing off a
telecommunications satellite. Eventually Parker said with
clear reluctance in his voice, "All right, Charlie. These
days I find I like the thought of sending you into danger
less and less."

"Sean never had a problem with that—before," I said
equably. "I suspect he'd have even less of a problem with
it now."

That brought another intake of breath and somewhere in there I could have sworn I heard an underlying wince.

"Well now, maybe that's something you need to get your head around," he said then. "For better or worse—I am not Sean."

Nineteen

WHEN I WALKED OUT of the hospital it was to find Joe Marcus waiting for me.

He was leaning against the front wing of a dirty white Toyota Land Cruiser, drinking from an insulated aluminium mug. As I neared I recognised the smell of strong coffee.

"Jump in," he said. "I'll give you a ride back to base."

"I didn't think the roads were clear enough to get through."

"Well, that was yesterday," he said. He peeled the top off his mug and threw away the dregs. "You all set?"

I shrugged and opened the passenger door while he got behind the wheel and cranked the engine.

"So, what did you get from him?" he asked as he swung the vehicle round in a wide circle and headed out.

"From the survivor? His name is Santiago Rojas—the owner of the jewellery store where we found him. He

101

reckons he was probably there alone when the quake hit. His memory's a little shaky, which is not surprising considering the crack on the head he took."

Marcus nodded briefly but there was something vaguely disapproving about him. I tried to work out if it was a general demeanour or if it was something I'd done—or might do. Well, if he was giving me the cold shoulder because he had a guilty conscience that was his problem.

The first half mile was slow. We were still moving through the city. Buildings had fallen sprawling across the roadway and had yet to be cleared. In places the road was only passable because the Toyota had four-wheel drive, all-terrain tyres and Joe Marcus had clearly driven off road before.

"Rojas thought he might know the couple we found nearby—that they might be customers. He said if that was the case the woman would be wearing a ruby engagement ring, and he asked if he could take a look at her, just to be sure."

"At the body?" Marcus shook his head. "Not happening," he said. "We learned a long time ago that visual identifications are a waste of time."

"Even by close relatives?"

"You got any siblings, Charlie?"

"No."

He gave a snort. "Figures," he said. "I got a brother I haven't seen for twenty years. I could walk right by him on the street and never know. For all I know he could have a shaved head, be covered in tattoos and every hole in his body pierced."

I didn't point out that apart from the silver in his hair and the lines cut deep around his eyes, Joe Marcus probably hadn't changed a bit in the last two decades. His brother, I decided, would know him anywhere.

"We tried visual IDs in the past," Marcus went on. "People are either so desperate for their loved ones to be found, dead or alive, that they'll claim anyone even vaguely similar, or they're in complete denial. Too many false positive and negatives."

"OK, that sounds logical, but can we at least check the woman's possessions for the ring he mentioned?"

"I'm sure that's one of the avenues Dr Bertrand will explore," he said and there was a finality to his words.

OK, that's me told.

I turned and stared out of the passenger window. Dusk was starting to fall hard, creating gloomy shadows from the ruined buildings. The streets were devoid of human life but we passed a pack of assorted dogs, half of which wore collars. They looked up hopefully and picked up their pace as we passed, like hitchhikers at the prospect of a ride, then fell away when we didn't stop. The animals would be as lost and confused as everyone else.

"You coping OK?" Marcus asked suddenly.

I turned back. "With what?"

"Your first day out there. Digging out the dead."

"And the living," I put in. I paused. "Tell me, did you ask Kyle Stephens the same question?"

His face gave a tic that might have signified irritation. "Meaning?"

"Meaning that do you think someone like Parker Armstrong would have sent me out here if he didn't know I could cope with whatever came up?"

"Everyone has their limits," Marcus said. "And yes, I did ask Kyle Stephens the same question."

Something in his voice alerted me. "But you didn't like his answer."

He glanced at me sharply then, no expression on his face. He had cool grey eyes very much like Parker's—a little darker maybe, a little closer to stone.

"Not much," he said. "It's a fine line we tread here between empathy and self-preservation. Some people have difficulty maintaining that balance."

And Stephens, I guessed, had been all about himself.

"You have to care, but not to the point of burn-out. I get that."

"You should do in your line of work," Marcus said. He flicked me another assessing look, only taking his eyes off the road for a second. "You lost a principal not so long ago."

That rocked me. "It happens. I'd be foolish to think it was never going to."

"Since then your boss, Sean Meyer, has not been back into the field," Marcus said, his neutral tone sending my heart rate rocketing, "but you have. And that makes me wonder which side of the line *you* tread."

"I care but I put it behind me and do my job—and technically he wasn't our principal," I said. "How do you know about that anyway?"

Marcus's voice hardened. "You think *I'd* let anyone just walk into *my* team without checking them out first?"

"No. I just didn't think you'd had the time."

"I made the time." He gave a dry smile. "And from what I hear, you'll go out on a limb for what you feel is right. That a fair assessment?"

"Pretty fair," I agreed.

"And who gets to choose what's right—you? What makes you qualified to make that decision?"

The intensity in him ensured I didn't come straight back with a glib reply. Eventually I said quietly, "Why not? You'd rather I abdicated responsibility to someone further up the line? So I could say, 'I was only following orders'?"

"But you're not much of one for following orders either, are you?"

"Depends on the orders—and who's giving them."

His fingers tightened on the rim of the Land Cruiser's steering wheel. "When I give an order I don't do it just to hear myself speak."

I recalled his order to Riley, back there above the fallen section of roadway, to put himself and his aircraft in serious jeopardy to effect a rescue that had turned out to be in vain anyway.

"Did Stephens follow orders?" I asked.

"Sometimes," Marcus returned. "When it mattered."

Hope had told me Stephens died because he didn't do what Joe Marcus told him. But given the number of conflicting stories I thought a fishing trip was worthwhile.

So I said, "Is that what he was doing when he died— following your orders?"

We'd cleared the city boundary now and were into an area that had escaped relatively undamaged. Marcus put his foot down and the Land Cruiser picked up speed.

"Kyle Stephens was a damned fool. He'd come through two Gulf Wars without a scratch and he thought he was indestructible," he said. "But are you asking me do I blame myself? Am I responsible for what happened? Then yes I am."

Twenty

IT WAS DARK by the time we got back to the army base. The gate sentry made a perfunctory check of our IDs and waved us through. Joe Marcus swung the Land Cruiser to a halt outside the mess hall and cut the engine. In the glare from the floodlighting the insects swirled as components of a larger mass.

"Grab some food, Charlie and get some rest," Marcus said. "It's been a long day and tomorrow won't be any shorter."

"I know," I said. "'The only easy day was yesterday', right?"

"You're thinking of the SEALs," he said, climbing out.

"Before we call it a day, I'd like to check on the items found with the woman—the one Rojas mentioned."

He turned back, flicking his head against the airborne bugs. Maybe that was why he looked annoyed to have his plans interrupted.

"I think Alex has her on tomorrow's list," he said. "What's the hurry?"

"There won't be time for me to wait around for the results in the morning, and I'd like to see her things—just in case the ring is there."

Or if it's been miraculously disappeared...

"Now?"

"Yes, now," I said, standing my ground. "If I'm going to call in on Rojas again on one of the hospital runs tomorrow, he'll want to know."

Marcus eyed me with a dispassionate gaze. "Chances are, by tomorrow, there won't be any more hospital runs," he said. "They'll all be coming here to the morgue."

"Even more reason not to leave it any longer than I have to then," I said. "You have a better idea?"

"Yeah," he said, exasperated. "Eating is a better idea than getting emotional over a piece of jewellery that still won't give us the woman's name."

"The credit card authorisation Rojas used will give us her name," I argued. "Five minutes is all I ask. In fact, all you need to do is unlock the door for me."

After another moment's grumpy silence Marcus let his breath out and reached into his pocket. He came out with a small bunch of keys which he threw across to me. I wasn't foolish enough to try to catch them, so I just stuck a foot out to stop them skidding off the path into the grass. You never knew what might be lurking there.

"Knock yourself out," Marcus said as I bent to retrieve the bunch. "Bring 'em back when you're done."

"Where will you be?"

He gave a now familiar snort as he turned away. "Eating," he said over his shoulder. "Where d'you think?"

I watched him walk away. Eating sounded like a very good idea, particularly as the smell of cooking drifted from the mess hall windows. If he hadn't been so stubborn I probably would have held off until morning but the more he'd tried to talk me out of the idea, the more important it seemed to find out the information tonight, dammit.

I headed in the opposite direction, trying to ignore the disaffected growling of my stomach.

Is that really what R&R did—robbed the dead of their belongings while they lay in cold storage nearby?

I thought again of those loose gems lying amid the broken glass outside the jewellery store. I wouldn't swear in court to the fact that their numbers had diminished in the time I'd been there, but it had certainly looked that way. The trouble was, it wasn't only R&R personnel who'd been on site. Any one of a host of other people, from the members of the dig team to the local police, could have pocketed a few stones in the time they were there. Perhaps it didn't feel like stealing if they were lying on full view in the street?

The lock to the hall being used as a makeshift mortuary had a piece of yellow insulating tape stuck underneath it. The same colour tape had been wrapped around the head of the key. An easily recognisable system that worked irrespective of language barriers. I felt the hand of Joe Marcus in there somewhere.

The key turned noiselessly in the lock. I opened the door and slipped inside, closing it again quietly behind me. Too much noise would have seemed disrespectful to the dead.

I paused just inside. Now I was there, alone and unsupervised, should I take the opportunity to have a nosy round? I smiled in the dark, mocking my own intent.

Yeah, Fox, and just what are you expecting to find? A treasure map with a convenient X marking the spot? A document marked 'Our Secret Plan'?

There was enough light coming in from outside that I didn't switch on the overhead lights. The personal possessions and clothing of the victims had been placed in archive boxes, all marked with a URN, and stored in an ante room off the main hall. The army had dragged in racking that, by the faint pervasive odour of gun oil still lingered around it, had once been used in their armoury.

I pushed open the dividing door and walked in. The windows were smaller in this room, and the height of the shelving made it darker still. I wasted time groping for a light switch I couldn't find. Eventually I gave up, standing for a moment in utter stillness, listening.

It was then I caught the thump of a full box dropping onto the hard tiled floor, and the scuffling sound of rapid footsteps.

Twenty-one

I TOOK A FIX on the direction of the sound and started running.

It was no surprise that the noise had come from the row housing the boxed possessions of the latest victims to be found. By the time I reached the end of the racking and catapulted around it, I'd just time to see a darkened figure disappearing at the far end. Automatically, I gave chase.

In the centre of the row was a mess of spilled boxes and their contents. I had to half step, half jump over the obstacle it created. Whatever they'd been looking for, our intruder had not been tidy about it. So, the object itself was more important than hiding the search. Or was this simple robbery?

As I pounded to the end of the row some sixth sense kicked in. I skidded to a halt just as a large fire extinguisher came swinging around the end of the racking. It hit the upright of the shelving unit a fraction of second before it would have connected with me, sending a reverberating clang through the whole length of it.

The intruder had put everything into his attack, relying on the weight and momentum of his chosen weapon to do the job for him. Missing had not been in the game plan. Neither was an opponent who didn't cower back after the first volley.

I'd learned a long time ago that even the most overwhelming odds can be successfully countered by speed and aggression. Now I used both, darting sideways and leaping to attack.

Even in the dark I managed to ram an elbow into the side of his neck just below his ear. He grunted in pain and stumbled forward. As he went down on his knees I spun, grabbed the back of his collar to locate him and kicked him in the ribs, my other arm outstretched for balance, giving it my all.

In the muted darkness I heard his breath explode out, heard the dull crack as a couple of ribs let go on his left-hand side. Still, he managed to fling his arm back, catching me low in the stomach with a clenched hammer-fist. It was only the pain from his busted ribs that took all the force out of the blow but it hurt enough to warn me to be careful of this man. He'd had training and he didn't give up easily.

I caught his flailing arm, hooked it up and back, starting to twist it into a lock. He countered by lurching sideways, despite the ribs, pivoted and kicked for my legs. I stamped on his ankle and booted him in the ribs again, eliciting an outraged squawk.

But just when I thought I might be winning fate threw a spanner in the works in the form of the fire extinguisher he'd used originally. By rolling him I'd inadvertently put it back within his reach. With a roar of pain and effort he grasped the metal cylinder, hoisted it overhead and hurled it straight at me like a medicine ball throw.

His aim was spoiled by his sudden inability to use his stomach muscles to their full potential. Even so, the cylinder weighed close to thirty-five pounds. It hit me low—across the chest rather than in the head as he'd no doubt intended—but hard enough to send me tumbling backwards.

I tucked and rolled, got my forearms up and mostly avoiding the damn thing landing directly on top of me. The extinguisher landed just below my sternum and toppled, skimming the side of my head as it went, rebounding off into the darkness.

Nevertheless, it knocked the wind out of me sufficiently to allow the intruder time to scramble to his feet and make a bolt for it. I heard him clatter away, gasping, while I took a vital couple of seconds to drag air into my spasmed diaphragm before I could follow.

Wary now of counterattack and with my head still ringing, I ran back through into the mortuary area taking great care at the doorway. I was slaloming between the empty stainless steel tables when I caught a peripheral glimpse of a figure sliding out of cover behind me. I crouched, had already started to turn when a voice cracked out:

"Hold it!"

And without needing to be told I knew the owner of that voice was either the best actor I'd ever come across, or he was holding a gun. There are not many people who can inject that kind of authority into their tone without firepower to back it up.

I froze, letting my hands come up and away from my sides to shoulder height. It was only then, as the red mist of combat dissipated like smoke, that I recognised the voice.

I let my hands drop back to my sides and turned around fully. "What the *hell* do you think you're doing, Marcus?"

He was indeed holding a gun, I saw, a big .45 calibre Colt 1911. It took him a moment to bring the muzzle up off target. He straightened out of a stance, relaxed his shoulders.

"I heard noise," he snapped. "What happened?"

"We *had* an intruder," I said, barely keeping hold of my temper. "But he'll be long gone by now."

"What was he after?"

I jerked my head back towards the ante room. "Come and see for yourself."

Marcus let the Colt drop alongside his leg, his finger outside the trigger guard, and followed me through. We split at the doorway—me heading left, him right. He found the switch for the overhead lights without difficulty. The rows of fluorescent tubes threw long shadows over the stacked boxes. Their significance as all that remained of the dead was suddenly very apparent to me.

I glanced along each row as I passed—saw Marcus doing the same thing at the far end—but everything was undisturbed until we came to the one housing the newest arrivals. I reached the mess of spilled boxes first and squatted on my haunches to survey the worst of it.

"This your doing?" Marcus asked.

I looked up sharply to find him approaching. He was carrying the errant fire extinguisher in one hand.

"Not exactly," I said, getting to my feet. "Although he threw it at me, if that's what you mean?"

Marcus put the cylinder down. It landed with a solid metallic thump on the hard floor. He moved forwards, eyes on me intently. I almost stepped back in response to the anger I saw there, had to force myself not to flinch when he reached for me.

"Let's see that." It was an order, not a request.

His fingers were cool against my cheek as he nudged my face to the side, angling it to the light. He wiped his thumb across the corner of my eyebrow and I felt the rasp of dried blood I hadn't realised was there.

"We should get that looked at," he said.

I shook myself out of his grasp. "Later. It's nothing," I said, ignoring the radiating headache. "It was a glancing blow. If he'd caught me full on I'd still be unconscious."

I'd once had my life saved by just such a fire extinguisher. I reckoned this made us even.

"Would you recognise him if you saw him again?"

"Probably," I said. "Depends if he bruises easily, but I broke at least two of his ribs, lower left. That's going to put a crimp in his day for a while."

Marcus's eyes narrowed as if trying to work out how much flippancy to ignore. Then he released me and nodded. "Good job."

"No, not really," I said grumpily. "If I'd done a good job I'd have him zip-tied face down on the floor right now and we'd know exactly what he was after."

Twenty-two

"**W**HY GO TO THE TROUBLE of breaking in 'ere to steal from the dead," Dr Bertrand demanded, "When we all know that items of value lie unguarded in the streets? It makes no sense."

She finished applying adhesive Steri-Strips to close the small cut to my eyebrow and stepped back with a nod of satisfaction at her own handiwork.

My smile of thanks went unacknowledged, so I asked, "Do we know which boxes were disturbed?"

Joe Marcus hesitated for a moment then said, "They targeted the people found close by where we pulled Santiago Rojas out of the jewellery store. The family in the car, the couple found outside the store, a man on the sidewalk, plus two more in an art gallery on the opposite side of the street."

"What was taken?"

He sighed. "That we don't know. It's all handwritten notes made by the recovery teams. Only as the victims are processed is everything photographed, formally catalogued and transferred to the computer system. There isn't time to do it in the field."

"Then they should make time!" Dr Bertrand said firmly. "As it is, we 'ave lost sources of valuable information. Without them, some of the identifications may be in doubt."

She was clearly taking this as a personal affront. I knew from the dossier Mrs Hamilton had provided on the R&R staff that the doctor prided herself on her track record when it came to reconciling the dead.

"Alex, it's close to a hundred degrees out there," Marcus said, his voice reasonable. "The longer it takes for the bodies to be gotten back here and into cold storage, the harder time you're gonna to have with 'em."

She gave a very Gallic shrug, stripped off her gloves and strode away across the deserted mortuary to replace the First Aid kit.

I hopped down from the steel post-mortem examination table where I'd been perched, and hoped it was a good few years before I found myself on one again.

As Dr Bertrand made her somewhat flouncy exit, Riley appeared with a stack of three archive boxes piled so tall in his arms he had to walk sideways to see where he was going. The muscles in his stringy biceps stood out starkly with the effort.

"That's everything gathered up," he said, dumping the boxes onto the table I'd just vacated. "He'd even ripped the inventory sheets off the outside of the boxes. Thorough bugger, wasn't he?"

"Not as thorough as he would have liked to be," I said. "Let's hope he left us *something* behind."

"Wallets and purses are gone," Riley said cheerfully. Most you've got is some jewellery and personal items."

"Is there a ruby engagement ring?" I asked. "It should have belonged to the woman from outside the jewellery store."

"Half a mo," Riley said, unstacking the boxes and removing the lid of the bottom one. He rummaged around inside, moving bags of clothing and shoes until he came to a bunch of smaller clear plastic zip-lock bags. I saw earrings in one, a thin gold watch, and finally a ring.

"How's that?" Riley handed it across. I looked through the plastic at the central stone. It was a beautiful deep clear red cut into a pointed oval and surrounded by smaller diamonds.

"I'm not an expert, but I'd guess that's a marquise-cut ruby," I said. "So if his memory was working right for that bit, we know this woman had just been into Rojas's store. If they paid by credit card there'll be an electronic trail with an ID at the end of it. Maybe we can trace her that way."

Joe Marcus had been looking through the box of items taken from the male victim found nearby. The bagged jacket and shirt, I noticed, were covered in darkly dried blood that gave them a similar tone to the ruby.

"No wallet for him, either," he said. He held another bag up for me to see. "Would you classify this as a fancy watch?"

I recognised the matte-black face and rubber strap. "I'll say. That's a Hublot, and they don't come cheap—ten grand at least."

Marcus frowned, unimpressed, and dropped the watch back into the box. "I'll take your word on that," he said. "Looks like we have a pair of tourists with more money than sense. Maybe somebody got wind of that and wanted what they had."

"So why take their IDs and leave the valuables behind?"

Riley laughed. "Because they weren't expecting to run into bloody Wonder Woman," he said. "You really reckon you bust the guy's ribs?"

"I heard them go." I kept my eyes on Marcus's face, wondering if he was going to mention the woman's wallet first, or whether I was going to have to bring it up. The latter, it seemed. "This wasn't the first attempt at taking the woman's ID, was it?" I murmured. "The police commander—Peck—he tried it, too. If it wasn't for it... falling out of his pocket when Lemon jumped up at him, it would have been in the hands of the police by now."

Marcus regarded me with a bland expression, refusing to rise to the bait.

"I'll contact him tomorrow and see if he remembers who she is. Meanwhile, Alex," he called across to where Dr Bertrand was jotting down notes for the morning's lists, "you better move these people up the priority lists. The woman especially."

"She was first on my list for tomorrow morning in any case," she agreed.

Marcus nodded, began to turn away when I stopped him with a question that should not have thrown him, given the circumstances.

"Does this kind of thing often—robberies from the dead?"

I saw the quick glance the three of them exchanged. It was Marcus who shook his head. "From our own morgue? Unheard of. And the curfews organised by the local police cut down on looting. Most people who break curfew are looking for missing family or pets."

"So there haven't been any recent cases?" I persisted.

"No." Another exchange of brief looks, more uneasy this time. "What are you getting at, Charlie?" Marcus asked, his tone a little harsh.

"Just trying to work out if there's a precedent," I said mildly, recognising that now was the time to back off a little. "If it's unusual then that makes it more significant, don't you think?"

He rolled his shoulders but they remained stiff. "Yeah, well, maybe I'll discuss that with Commander Peck tomorrow." He stepped back, gestured for all of us to head for the door. "Now let's get some rest, people. One way or another, we're gonna need it."

It was only as he pulled the door to the mortuary shut behind us and twisted the key in the lock that I voiced my final point.

"One thing worth bearing in mind for tomorrow," I said. He paused, raised an eyebrow. "When you ask Commander Peck about this mystery woman, you might want to check if any of his ribs are broken..."

Twenty-three

I SPENT the following morning combing another shopping district with Hope and Lemon. We discovered and marked the location of a further four bodies. There were no more live finds.

The general feeling among the dig teams was that we'd now moved on to the recovery stage of the operation. They were matter-of-fact but subdued about it. Didn't stop them running whenever they thought there might be a possibility, though. A triumph of hope over experience.

I was expecting to put in another long day so it was a surprise when I heard rotors sweep low overhead and recognised the R&R Bell circling as Riley picked his landing spot.

He put the helo down in the middle of a car park, one side of which had disappeared into a crater, and came jogging across. In the short time I'd known the laidback Aussie, I'd never seen him look in such a hurry.

"Hey Riley," Hope called. "Where's the fire?"

"G'day, ladies," he called back with a grin. "How's it going?"

"Depends on your point of view, I think," I said. I nodded to the line of body bags. "If you're heading back to base we've four passengers for you."

"Better make that seven," Riley said. "Joe Marcus wants you back at the morgue right away. And Hope—and her ladyship of course."

"What for?"

He shrugged. "I'm just the oily rag, sweetheart, not the engine driver."

Hope appeared by my shoulder with Lemon at her side. "So, what's the rush?" she asked. "Lem's on a roll."

He shrugged. "All I know is, the boss said it was urgent. And when he speaks I don't argue."

The on-site dig team—mostly from New Zealand where they'd gained their experience during the 2011 Christchurch quake—helped us load the body bags into the Bell. Hope and I climbed aboard without speaking and Lemon jumped in, turned around twice and plonked herself down at Hope's feet. She seemed unfazed by her proximity to so much dead meat.

It didn't take long to get back to the army base. Nowhere takes long when you can take a crow-flies route and don't ever meet traffic. But all the way there I tried to work out the reason for this abrupt summons.

Do they know why I'm really here? And if so, how did they find out? Or did they guess?

Perhaps my question about the frequency of thefts from the dead had struck too close to home. But with no sign of obvious forced entry to the morgue or the ante room, it was looking decidedly like either a pro at work or an inside job.

I half expected to find Joe Marcus waiting on the landing pad with my kitbag at his feet and an instruction not to bother getting out because I was on my way straight back to the airport.

But the only people waiting for us when we set down were the army stretcher teams—Riley must have radioed ahead. Between us we quickly offloaded our cargo.

It was Hope who looked about her, puzzled, and said, "Are you going to go find Joe? I want to know what's worth dragging us off site in the middle of the day. He wants his bumps feeling for that."

I agreed, even if I wasn't going to volunteer to be the one to do it. I asked one of the stretcher bearers if they'd seen Joe Marcus and was told he was in the morgue with Dr Bertrand.

Hope pulled a face and said she'd take Lemon to the mess hall and see what they could scrounge between them.

"You'll come and find me when you're done with Joe?" she asked.

I assured her I would.

I found Marcus in the mortuary as predicted, together with Dr Bertrand and, to my surprise, the police commander, Peck. The two men were standing back from one of the post-mortem exam tables, watching Dr Bertrand peeling open the chest of a lean male cadaver. His face was a mess, crushed and misshapen, the features offset as if wearing a horror mask that had badly slipped.

It was damage I recognised.

"Ah, Charlie," Marcus said when he caught sight of me, adding dryly, "You already met Commander Peck, I understand."

"Yes sir," I said, holding my hand out as I approached. Automatic good manners had Peck reaching to shake it. I gave it a few hearty pumps with a friendly smile on my face, watching him for signs of discomfort. He showed only bemusement at my enthusiastic greeting.

Damn. That's that theory out the window.

Marcus gestured to the body on the slab. "This is the guy who—"

"Was found outside the jewellery store with the woman," I finished for him. "Yes, I know."

He raised an eyebrow.

It was Peck who demanded, "You *know* this man?"

"Not his identity, no. But I got a good look at him yesterday...when you were searching the bodies after they were brought out," I said. "It's not a state of face you forget in a hurry."

Dr Bertrand glanced at the body with a frown, as if unable to work out what made it memorable. I guessed she'd seen a lot worse in her time.

"That is immaterial," she said. She indicated the gaping chest cavity with a gore-spattered glove. "What I found 'ere is of greater concern at present. See for yourself."

The invitation was issued in an off-hand manner with just an underlying hint of smug. She clearly expected me not to spot whatever it was she was indicating. Then I would be compelled to ask and she would have the opportunity to sledgehammer home her superior knowledge.

I moved closer, leaned over the body, remembering to breathe shallowly through my mouth. It didn't stop the taste of death from settling on my tongue but it was better than the alternative.

Looking down, I saw the rib cage had already been cracked open and the breastplate of sternum and ribs removed in one piece. The heart and other organs still nestled in place but I noticed a blackened torn mass at the bottom edge of the left lung. I peered closer, then glanced up and met Dr Bertrand's quickly hidden look of surprise.

"Would you mind, doctor?" I asked politely, indicating the lower triangular flap of skin that she had folded back to hide the whole of the abdomen. With disapproval in every line, she lifted it for me to inspect. I saw what I was looking for almost at once, nodded and stepped back.

"He was shot," I said, drawing blank stares from the three of them. Not for my verdict but the fact I'd been able to reach it.

Twenty-four

"**Y**OU CAN SEE the front entry wound—here," I said, keeping my voice cool and level, pointing to the dead man's chest. "I'd say the round clipped the bottom edge of his lung. Without taking a look at his back I wouldn't like to guess on it being a through-and-through but it wasn't a large calibre if I'm any judge—maybe a thirty-eight or a nine mil. The wound was possibly not bad enough to be immediately fatal, but without immediate medical attention I doubt he would have lasted long."

And he didn't last long because—looking at his face— the earthquake got him before he had a chance to bleed out or suffocate to death.

For a second nobody moved and then Dr Bertrand gave me a stiff little nod, as if it grieved her to have to do it.

Commander Peck cleared his throat. "We are looking at homicide here and I shall be launching a full investigation."

125

"Maybe, maybe not," Joe Marcus said. "If the quake hadn't hit, he might have survived."

"With a bullet through his lung?" Peck scoffed.

"Why not?" I asked. "I managed just that a year or so ago. I have the scars to prove it."

Peck gave me a strange look as if he was pretty sure I was joking but he couldn't be sure. "Either way, you don't shoot a man in the chest without intending to kill him, regardless of what actually finishes him off."

I couldn't refute the logic of that. "Do we know who he is yet?"

Marcus lifted one shoulder. "Maybe," he said. "The woman he was found with is a French tourist, Gabrielle Dubois. According to immigration, she entered the country last weekend, travelling with a man called Enzo Lefévre, her fiancé."

"That was quick," I said.

Marcus ducked his head in Peck's direction. "The commander remembered her name from looking at her ID," he said without inflection. "From there it was easy enough to check out her passport record."

I nodded, turning over this new information. If Peck had originally taken the woman's wallet to conceal her identity, why give it up voluntarily now? After all, it would have been entirely believable for him to say he didn't take a good enough look at the ID to recall the details.

"You seemed to think she'd been reported missing. Was that why you were looking for her?" I asked him.

He lifted a casual shoulder. "I thought I recognised her but I was mistaken." His face was expressionless, giving nothing away. Probably best never to get into a poker game with the police commander.

"So...why drag us off the streets for this?" I asked Marcus, getting the perplexity into my voice without having to work too hard. "Couldn't it have waited until we got back later?"

His face ticked in irritation. "Because there's a threat here you need to be aware of, Charlie," he said. "Somebody shot this guy right before the earthquake hit. We don't know why, and we haven't yet recovered a body clutching a gun. Plus there were no survivors other than the store owner on that street, so it looks like our gunman got away."

"He could well be the man you say broke in here last night," Peck said. "Although I have inspected all the points of entry and can only assume this man was highly professional, or that he had access."

It was an echo of my own earlier thoughts, and although he left that one dangling nobody wanted to make a grab for it.

"So, why steal their identification?" I asked instead. "What does that achieve?"

"Perhaps the robber was known to them." Peck made a vague flapping motion with his hand. "Perhaps he fears that if we were able to identify these people we might also make some connection to him?"

Marcus's stare lasted a second or two longer than it needed to, and spoke volumes as to what he thought of that idea.

"Or perhaps," I echoed the commander with a straight face, "Mr Rojas might be able to fill in some blanks."

Peck straightened to show the mild jibe had not passed unnoticed. "I will be questioning Rojas in due course. I trust that you will leave this in my hands." He gave a stilted bow of his head to Dr Bertrand and Joe Marcus but ignored me completely as he headed for the main door out of the mortuary.

"You know, Charlie," Marcus said as we watched the commander disappear. "I get the feeling he really doesn't like you."

"Oh-dear-what-a-pity-never-mind," I said cheerfully. "So, when do we go and see Mr Rojas?"

Just for a second Marcus's severe face cracked into a smile. "Any time you're ready."

"I'll just go and let Hope know what's happening," I said. "I'll meet you by the helo in five."

But Hope was not in the mess hall as I expected. I jogged across the parade square to the NCOs' quarters we'd been assigned, aware that if I went more than half a minute past the five I'd promised Marcus, he was likely to take off without me.

That was the reason I forgot my manners and just shoved open the door to Hope's room already calling her name.

And my voice died in my throat.

Hope was sitting cross-legged on her bed. Her head jerked up when I burst in and her mouth formed a soundless oh. Spread on a shirt in front of her was a pile of stones. Some of them were pebbles, of the type that I'd seen Lemon delivering to her so solemnly when we were out in the field.

But the others were far too small to have been picked up by a dog's mouth, however delicate. They glittered against the fabric, cut and graded and polished—the precious stones I'd seen scattered outside Santiago Rojas's jewellery store.

Hope tensed, her eyes darted wildly. They even flicked to where Lemon lay stretched out on a blanket with her favourite chew toy next to her. The yellow Lab had lurched from her side onto her belly when I made my entrance, letting out a couple of loud sneezes as she was woken from sleep. She lifted her head, recognised me and flopped back down again with a loud grumbling sigh.

Hope's flight reflex folded in on itself and collapsed, taking her composure with it. For a moment I thought she might cry.

I stood there frozen with one hand still on the door-knob until I heard footsteps and voices approaching. I stepped inside quickly and closed the door.

"What's going on, Hope?" I asked, keeping my voice calm and quiet. I'd seen how Lemon leapt to her handler's defence when it was clear the girl was being threatened and I had no desire to be on the receiving end of those teeth.

Hope bounced off the bed, tangling her bare feet in the blankets and stumbling straight into my arms in her haste.

"Please," she said, staring up at me. "Please, Charlie, don't tell anyone!"

"Hope..." My voice trailed away helplessly. I shook my head, said tiredly, "Just tell me what the hell is going on, will you?"

That seemed to get to her more than harsh words would have done. She wrenched herself away and slumped down on the edge of the bed with her head bowed. Lemon rolled partly onto her back and gazed up at her with two legs waving and her tongue hanging out. Hope rubbed the side of the dog's belly with one foot.

"You picked these up on the street, didn't you?" I went on when she didn't speak. Let Joe Marcus go without me if he damn well pleased. As far as I was concerned this took precedence. Still, I didn't have all night. "Hope?"

"Yes," she said, lifting her head and showing me more than a hint of defiance. "They're just lying there, for fuck's sake. Anybody could help themselves. You think they'll be any left by the time that jeweller gets clearance to go back?"

"That doesn't mean they're yours to take," I said neutrally.

"Why not?" she cried. "I've seen everyone take things, even the cops. Even the birds!" She let her head drop again so her next words emerged as a mumble: "S'not like I was gonna keep them."

I opened my mouth to make a "yeah, right" kind of comment, but then I remembered again the way she'd put the woman's wallet back after she'd lifted it from Commander Peck and I stopped myself from coming out with anything too cynical.

"Who knows about this?" I asked instead.

"Nobody!" she assured me. If she kept bobbing her head up and down like this she was going to put her neck out. "Nobody else knows about it, and nobody else is doing it. It's just me, all right?"

I took in her mulish expression and realised there was no point arguing with her. Not right now. I checked my watch. "Look, Hope, I'm going back to see the jewellery store owner—"

"Oh, please don't tell him! I'll put them all back, I swear!"

I let my breath out. "I wasn't going to tell him," I said. "I simply meant I haven't time to talk about this now, but we *are* going to talk about it—later, when I get back, yes?"

Another mumble, less distinct this time. I took it for a yes anyway.

"Good," I said. I reached for the door handle again, paused as a final thought struck me. "Did Kyle Stephens know you were helping yourself to bits and pieces?"

Hope didn't answer that one, but from the sudden flare of loathing and fear that crossed her face, I didn't need her to.

Twenty-five

I WAS, I REALISED as Joe Marcus and I headed back towards the hospital with Riley in the Bell, getting far too used to travelling everywhere by helicopter. Being grounded was going to seem very restrictive after all this.

What I needed was to get out on a fast bike on an open road and blow the cobwebs out of my head. I still hadn't replaced my Buell Firebolt after it was written-off by a bunch of kidnappers. Sean's own bike remained under a cover in the parking garage below our building. I thought longingly of the Honda FireBlade I'd left behind in the UK, sitting equally dormant in the back of my parents' garage. Maybe I'd get over there this year and take it out for a blast—if the tyres weren't flat-spotted with standing and the fuel left in the tank hadn't gone off.

Or maybe not.

Unable to side-track myself any longer, I dragged my mind back to Hope Tyler. I knew I was putting off examining what I'd seen and heard, and what it might mean. Hope was a confirmed thief, no two ways about it. She was too quick with her fingers to be anything else and it would seem that she'd trained Lemon to aid and abet. I wondered what the RSPCA or PETA would have to say about that.

Still, if Hope had been helping herself from other disaster sites, would that really be enough to cause the rumours Mrs Hamilton had heard all the way back in New York? Hope struck me as a collector of pretty things rather than a serious player, but that didn't mean she hadn't tried to offload some of her booty in search of yet more pretty things. Wouldn't take much carelessness there for her activities to come to light.

Kyle Stephens had known what was going on—that much was clear from her reaction. When had he found out, and what had he been intending to do about it? I got the impression from Mrs Hamilton that what she really wanted was not confirmation or denial of the thefts, but for the problem to be simply made to go away. She had asked Stephens to take care of it for her.

Instead he'd got himself killed.

I was still tumbling those thoughts over and round when Riley set the Bell down on the pad outside the hospital and the engines spun down.

"I never trust a woman when she goes quiet," Joe Marcus said as we hopped down onto the baked concrete. "What's on your mind, Charlie?"

"Life, death, the universe and everything," I said, keeping my tone light. "Any clues?"

"Given some thought to all of it over the years."

"And?"

He shook his head. "Never did come to any conclusions worth a damn."

We found Santiago Rojas looking both better and worse.

Better because he was out of his hospital bed and sitting in a low chair by the window. Worse because the bruising had blossomed across his face, turning his skin every colour of pain. He shifted awkwardly when we entered, making as if to rise. Marcus waved him back into his seat.

I introduced them. Rojas clasped Marcus's hand warmly, his eyes becoming moist. "So, you are one of the people responsible for getting me out of there alive," he said, his voice husky. "For that, sir, I am forever in your debt."

"It's kinda the whole point of what we do," Joe Marcus said without any hint of embarrassment. I guessed he'd received a lot of similar thanks in his time.

"I would like to give you something," Rojas went on. "A small gift, from my store. Something of value—"

"That won't be necessary," Marcus said quickly, and I couldn't help wondering what he might have said if I hadn't been with him. "If you feel you'd like to make a contribution to one of the disaster relief funds, well that would be more than enough."

"Ah, of course," Rojas said quickly, not wanting to cause offence. His eyes went from one of us to the other expectantly.

"We wondered if you'd had any more recollections of what happened—just before the earthquake?" I said.

He frowned. "I do not understand why it is so important for you to know this," he said. "There must be so many dead and injured."

"You remember the couple I told you about? They were found just outside your store—the woman with the ruby engagement ring?"

"Ah, you found the ring. So it is her?" He nodded sadly. "I am so sorry they did not survive. She was so beautiful. And she seemed so happy."

"Her name was Gabrielle Dubois," Marcus said. "What can you tell us about the man who was with her?"

"Her fiancé?" Rojas gave a confined shrug, as much as his injuries would allow. "He was a man of...sophistication. A man of the world, I think you would say. Older than she, but good-looking, of course, to have snared such a beautiful lady."

"Mr Rojas, our doctor has just carried out an autopsy on this man—we believe his name is Enzo Lefévre. He was shot in the chest shortly before the earthquake struck," Marcus said gravely. "Would you happen to recall anything about that?"

His level tone and gaze would have been enough to make a nun confess, but Rojas just stared with his mouth slightly agape.

"Shot?" he repeated. "Holy Mother of God..." His focus went into middle distance as if trying to latch onto a fragment of memory. Eventually he murmured, "So, *that* was it."

"That was what?" Marcus demanded.

Rojas pulled his attention back onto us with an effort. "I've been having...strange dreams," he said hesitantly. "Of violence, of someone crying out, of a loud noise and fear and falling. I thought...I thought it was all to do with the earthquake, with being buried, but now..."

"Now?" Marcus prompted.

He was not the subtlest of interrogators but his technique seemed to work because a moment later Rojas said, more firmly, "Now I believe that, just before the earth opened up and swallowed me...I believe I was robbed."

Twenty-six

"**I** REMEMBER THE COUPLE coming into the store," Rojas said. "They said they had just become engaged—that he had asked her only that morning, and she had said yes. She was still blushing, so pretty."

"Just that morning?" I queried and he nodded.

I was sure Peck had said Gabrielle Dubois was listed as travelling with her fiancé on the flight details. Perhaps it was just easier that way. In the past I'd wondered how I should introduce Sean. He was too old to be called "boyfriend", too practical be described as "lover", but the all-encompassing "partner" sounded so soulless.

It was all a bit of a moot point now...

"How long were they in the store?" Joe Marcus asked.

"Oh, almost an hour. She tried on a great many beautiful rings before she settled on the marquise-cut ruby. It was an exquisite stone. And the size, it was perfect for her. She said it was a sign that she was meant to have it."

His eyes began to fill again. Marcus said, "Take your time, Mr Rojas."

I plucked a handful of tissues from the box on the bedside cabinet and passed them across. Rojas took them with a nod of thanks.

"The doctors tell me it is the...relief of my rescue still coming out," he explained and we didn't call him a liar.

"Do you remember anything about the robbery itself?" Marcus asked after a few moments. I raised an eyebrow at him. What part of *"take your time"* did this fit into?

But Rojas was nodding. "Yes...yes, I think so. I have a remote lock on the door. I would have had to press it to let the couple out. I think that was when the man pushed his way inside. He pushed them back inside, also. He wore black, and a mask. And he had a gun. He forced me to open my gem safe. He threatened the lady...what could I do?"

"I'm sure you did everything you could," Marcus murmured.

"He was expecting more stones. I was waiting for a shipment, but it was delayed. I tried to explain but he was very angry. Eventually he took what he could, including the cash in the register, and just when I thought he might finally leave, he saw the woman's ring—the ruby. And he wanted it."

"And Monsieur Lefévre didn't want to let go of it," Marcus guessed.

Rojas nodded helplessly, his English breaking up in his distress. "He shoot him in the chest and he go. And then the building start to shake and I...I don't remember much after that."

He sagged back into his chair as if the retelling of the tale had physically exhausted him. I sat quiet for a moment, lining his story up with the holes in our own timeline. It would all seem to fit except for the unknown intruder who'd broken in to steal the couple's identities—and from a secure building in the middle of an army base at that.

I still didn't see the point of it. Unless Peck had been right and there *was* some connection between the couple and the robber that he thought too obvious to risk exposing.

"Do you have any ideas who might have robbed you?" I asked. "Or if there might have been any connection between the couple who came in, and the robbery?"

"How could there be, when he shoot that man?" Rojas demanded.

I exchanged a look with Joe Marcus, saw no enlightenment in his face either. Perhaps I needed to get Parker Armstrong digging on the French pair to see what he could come up with.

We got to our feet. Marcus reached a hand to Rojas, who clasped it again briefly, and did the same with mine.

"Well, thank you for your time and your patience, Mr Rojas," Marcus said. "We hope—"

"What in the name of hell is going on here?" said an annoyed voice from the doorway. Commander Peck came striding into the room and stopped dead when he caught sight of the man in the chair, his head bruised and still swathed in dressings.

"Ah, Commander Peck, is it not?" Rojas said, and there was a rueful note to his smile. "My name is Santiago Rojas. I believe you want to speak with me."

"Mr Rojas," Peck returned, so stiffly it made his treatment of us seem positively effusive. Enmity rolled off him like cold air from an open fridge door.

"You must excuse us, Mr Marcus, Miss Fox," Rojas said then, a bitter smile curving his swollen lips. "I'm afraid the commander and I have some...history together, is that not right?"

Peck said nothing.

Rojas laughed. "The good commander works long hours," Rojas went on, "and his wife is a lonely and attractive woman." He shrugged as far as he was able.

"Our...friendship was over some time ago, but I think I am not yet forgiven."

Peck forced some of the rigidity out of his shoulders and jaw. "Our personal...differences will not prevent me from doing my job," he ground out. "You can be assured of that."

Twenty-seven

"**W**E'RE WORKING IN THE DARK," Marcus said when we were outside and heading for the Bell.

"You should be used to that in your job," I said, which raised the beginnings of a smile that never made it any further. "Why don't you check with your sources—see what they have to say?"

"My sources?"

"You found out all the gory details about me fast enough after I arrived," I pointed out mildly. "You must have a good source of intel somewhere along the line."

"Good, yes," he agreed. "Sporadic, also. And right now my 'source' as you call him, is on deployment and out of regular cellphone contact."

"Well, it's fortunate that *my* source is sitting by his phone in New York," I said. "I can ask my boss to do some digging on this if you want?"

"We talking about Sean Meyer?" he demanded. "Or Parker Armstrong?"

My hesitation was only fractional. "Parker."

He regarded me for a moment and I could see the pros and cons circulating behind those stony eyes before he said, "Do it."

I pulled my cellphone out of my pocket and hit the speed dial number for Parker's direct line. He picked up on the third ring—a slow response for him.

"Charlie, how's it going?"

"Fairly quiet," I said, which he knew meant the opposite. I watched Joe Marcus walk over to Riley, who was fussing with the tensioning of the winch he'd reinstalled. "You got anything for me?"

"We looked into the girl," he said cautiously. "No record, not even a parking ticket. Although as she doesn't have a driving licence maybe that's not so hard to believe. No late payments, no final demands, no credit card. The kid's practically a ghost."

"Hmm," I said. "Can I ask you to take another run at that?"

I almost heard his ears prick up. "Ah. Developments?"

"On that front, yes and I'll fill you in when I can," I said. "But there have been other developments, too." And I told him briefly about the robbery of Santiago Rojas's store, the dead French couple, and the intruder at the mortuary who'd stolen their IDs—and whose ribs I'd busted.

"This sounds like the kind of thing the local LEOs should be handling," Parker said when I was done. "It's way outside your remit."

"You know the scope of my remit as well as I do, Parker," I countered. "Besides, there was no forced entry into the mortuary—"

"Which means we can't rule out an inside job," he finished for me wearily. "Yeah, OK. I'll do what I can."

"Besides which," I added, "I don't entirely trust the local head honcho. For a while I thought he might even be our intruder. I can rule him out personally, but that doesn't mean he didn't get one of his boys to indulge in a bit of Breaking and Entering on the side. I can't go around hugging all of them to find out."

I still had my eyes on Joe Marcus, apparently shooting the breeze with Riley, both of them casual and relaxed. But just as Parker's voice in my ear asked, "So, are they still... treating you OK?" both men seemed to glance over in my direction at the same time. The look they gave me was anything but warm and fuzzy.

"For the moment at least," I said carefully. "Which is lucky really, because if they decide I need to follow in my predecessor's footsteps, so to speak, I don't think I'd get much backup from the local cops."

"Are you trying to give me grey hair, Charlie?"

"Parker, your hair's been grey practically since you were in short trousers—I've seen the pictures."

"Yeah, and that means I don't want it to start falling out from stress," he returned. "Watch your step and I'll get back to you as soon as I can, OK?"

I ended the call and ambled towards Riley and Marcus. Riley was wiping his hands on an old rag while the former Marine had donned a pair of heavy gloves and was trying the winch line to make sure it ran out and retracted smoothly.

"Well?" Marcus wanted to know as soon as I reached them.

"He's checking," I said. "As soon as I know anything I'll pass it on."

He gave a grumpy kind of a sigh at that, as though he'd heard such promises many times before and knew they rarely came to fruition.

"OK, Riley," he called to the Bell pilot. "We're good to go."

"Hop in then, mate," Riley said with a grin. "Now I've got the winch hunky dory I can set you down any place you fancy."

Marcus glanced at me. "Well, Charlie? You up for finding out what happened to that gun?"

I shrugged. "What's so important about this one? There must be thousands of weapons loose in this city right now."

"Thousands? Maybe," he agreed, "but not many we know for certain have been used as a murder weapon."

"There are plenty with the potential to kill far more."

"Maybe," he repeated. "You have that same potential but I'm not chasing you."

I opened my mouth to voice another objection then closed it again. Joe Marcus was suddenly very insistent to go back to the scene of the crime and all of a sudden I could think of several reasons for that which had nothing to do with a missing gun. What better way to find out?

I climbed into the back of the Bell without comment. It meant I couldn't see their faces easily. At least I didn't have the former Marine sitting behind me. Marcus took the co-pilot's seat. It wasn't until we were in the air that I spoke into the boom mic attached to my headset.

"If he got away clear before the quake hit, there won't be any weapon to find."

Marcus looked back over his shoulder. "And if he didn't?"

"Then Hope and Lemon would have found his body."

Marcus tilted his head and his mouth twitched. "They're good, Charlie, but they're not infallible."

"In that case," I said carefully, "I don't suppose this additional search might have anything to do with a bag of missing diamonds, would it?"

This time Joe Marcus didn't turn his head so I couldn't see his expression. He and the Aussie didn't even glance at each other. After a moment Marcus said, "If it's missing, that means it can be found."

"Possibly a lot of money's worth there." I tried to keep my voice casual, as if I were seriously considering this. "You thinking there might be a reward?"

"Possibly." He echoed me in both tone and caution.

I pursed my lips even though he couldn't see me, knowing it would affect my voice just the same. "Slim chance," I said. "Do you honestly think Rojas has had time to even report the robbery yet? The man's still in hospital. He hasn't been back to the store to do an inventory—even if he was allowed near the place, never mind inside."

"I'm sure they take that into account."

"Will they? Or will they simply declare this whole mess an Act of God or whatever the terminology is and void everyone's insurance?"

"For property damage, they might," Marcus returned, "but according to Rojas the robbery took place before the earthquake hit. In theory he'd still be covered."

"Yeah, because we all know how honest and fair-dealing insurance companies are," I said sarkily.

I caught his smile, a flash of surprisingly white teeth. "You always look on the downside, Charlie?"

"It's part of my job description." I paused, decided to edge this forward just a touch. "Rojas said he was waiting for a big shipment that was delayed," I added, aiming for a note of calculation. "You really think there's enough out there to get excited about?"

Marcus shrugged, not taking the bait. "Let's see if we can find the gun first and talk about anything else later."

Damn. Ah well, may as well be hanged for a sheep as a lamb...

"Why don't you put your cards on the table, Joe," I said. "Are you thinking of handing those gems in for the reward—assuming there is one—or are you thinking instead of not handing them in at all?"

It took him a beat or two before he answered. "I can think of a whole heap of better uses for them than left lying around in the street."

It was within a hairsbreadth of an admission, but not quite all the way there yet. I knew I needed to push just that little bit further.

"So, how many ways are you thinking of splitting it?"

Again came the little tilt of his head. The one that told me nothing. "This was your idea, Charlie, not mine," he said. "What exactly did you have in mind?"

"Hey, I'm just the newbie," I said with as much unconcern as I could muster. "How do you usually work it?"

Marcus was silent for a moment, then said with icy disdain, "I wonder what the illustrious Mrs Hamilton would have to say about your suggestion. But I'll wager this was not quite what she had in mind when she went to Armstrong-Meyer for Stephens' replacement."

"If you kids can stop haggling long enough to grab your gear," Riley cut in from the pilot's seat, "we're coming up on your search location now." There was little to be gleaned from his voice to know if he was for or against the idea of keeping the missing gems.

"Set us down where you can," Joe Marcus said, turning all business once again. I cursed long and silently behind a bland expression. If he knew who had gone to Parker, and why, then I was probably blown from the start. No wonder Riley had tried to shake me off the skid of the Bell on the very first day.

The Aussie made another deceptively casual landing and was in the air again as soon as we'd jumped down into the rubble. He hovered through our standard radio checks, then moved off with a jaunty wave through the canopy.

I returned the salute and watched him surf the rooftops until the Bell disappeared from view. As the thrum of the rotors began to fade into the distance I started to turn back to Joe Marcus. And as I did so I heard the unmistakable harsh metallic click of the slide being racked back to chamber the first round into the breech of a semiautomatic.

Twenty-eight

I COMPLETED MY TURN very slowly and found Joe Marcus with that big Colt .45 in his hands again. The only thing that kept my heartrate from going stratospheric was the fact the gun wasn't pointing at me.

Marcus was wearing a loose shirt over khaki cargoes but I hadn't picked up any sense that he was armed. Which meant either he was really good, or I was slipping. And as before I knew that he didn't carry just for show—he was more than capable of using.

The SIG sat snug in the small of my back under my own shirt. I knew I could get to it quickly but not quickly enough.

"You expecting to repel boarders?" I asked with a calm I did not feel.

He stared at me for a moment with no humour in his face. I fought to keep my shoulders easy and my hands relaxed by my sides. Then he tucked the Colt away under his shirt again and moved past me.

"No point in carrying a weapon that isn't ready to shoot," he said. He paused, found me still frozen. "You coming or what?"

"'What', probably," I muttered and followed him.

We picked our way over the rubble until we turned into the street where Lemon had found Santiago Rojas. Another building had partially come down during the night. We were getting perhaps half a dozen aftershocks a day, some worse than others. Unless they threatened to throw me off my feet I tended to ignore them. How quickly we learn to be blasé.

"So, if we're searching for something specific why didn't you bring Hope along?"

Marcus stepped across an eighteen-inch gap in the road surface without apparent concern.

"It's not exactly Lemon's specialty," he said.

"Oh I don't know. Hope reckons once that dog's had a sniff of just about anything she can find it again."

"Yeah, well, they both do enough to earn their keep," Marcus said with a flick of irritation in his voice. "And maybe I don't want to expose the kid to danger unnecessarily."

"She's an adult, as she's only too ready to point out. She's capable of making her own choices." I thought of the gems I'd seen Hope inspecting in the privacy of her room and added silently, *however poor some of those choices might be.*

He hesitated and a dark flicker crossed his features. "In many ways she's still a child. And she's on my team—my responsibility."

That hesitation made me curious. Time to push it again, gun or no gun.

"So, do you take responsibility for her actions too?"

Joe Marcus stopped then, turned to look back at me with his head tilted in a manner I was coming to know well. For a moment I thought I might be getting somewhere. "Might be easier if we split up," he said then. "Keep your radio on. If you find anything, call me."

"Likewise."

"Of course."

I watched him walk away, hopping nimbly over tumbled blockwork and daggers of broken glass still fettered to their twisted wooden frames.

"Yeah," I said quietly, "I bet you will..."

I headed for the nearest cross-street, a wider main road that bisected the tourist district. From there I cut down the service road running behind Rojas's jewellery store. In the mouth of the narrow street I halted, trying to get a feel for my quarry's train of thought.

The main road would have been a faster escape route for our gem thief but it was also more exposed. If I'd been him I would have stuck to the alleyways until I was well clear, but if he had enough bottle he could have shed his mask and gloves, disguised his booty in a brightly coloured shopping bag and strolled away like any other tourist. A studied lack of urgency would have proved very effective camouflage.

And this was a man, after all, who had robbed a high-end jewellery store, alone in broad daylight. Surely he must have known that as soon as he was out of the door Rojas would be straight on the phone to the cops—whatever his relationship with Peck might have been.

Unless, of course, the unlucky Frenchman was not the only person the robber had been intending to leave behind him dead.

Logic told me the man was long gone but that didn't stop me from reaching very quietly under the back of my shirt and easing the pistol grip of the SIG into my palm. It said something about what my life had become that I always felt better with a gun in my hand.

Maybe that was one of the many things that had driven Sean away.

I shook my head as if to dispel flies. Now was not the time. *When is?*

Besides, the unknown robber was not the only person who might have a reason for wanting me out of the way.

I approached the shadowed service road in the same way I would a live-firing Close Quarter Battle range, moving quiet and cautious. I put my feet down with great care, making sure each step was solid before I trusted my weight to it, just in case I had to launch for cover. I led with the gun in both hands, my right forefinger close but off the trigger. Aware of their precarious nature I avoided hugging the buildings too much, instead spending as much time with my eyes on possible hiding places as searching the ground.

Nobody leapt out at me and I found nothing.

I had almost reached the end and was already mentally tossing a coin for right or left when the radio came to life in my earpiece.

"Charlie, you read me?"

I settled the SIG into my right hand and reached for the transmit button with my left.

"I'm here, Joe. Go ahead."

His next transmission was indistinct. I halted, frowning, thumbed up the volume on my handset.

"Say again?"

"I asked if you were due east of our insertion point?" His voice came over louder this time but I got the impression he was speaking softly.

I took a few paces forward so I was just out of the service road and glanced up at the sun, shielding my eyes. After some quick ready reckoning of direction I hit transmit again, swinging round as I did so. After the relative gloom of the service road it was uncomfortably bright out there.

"Negative. More like southwest."

"In that case—"

He never got to finish whatever he'd been about to say. At that moment a high-pitched whine zinged past my ear. The brickwork within a couple of feet of where I'd been standing disintegrated with a sharp, vicious crack.

Twenty-nine

I TWISTED on the balls of my feet and threw myself sideways, back toward the relative safety of the service road entrance. Another round followed the first. If I hadn't moved instantly, that one would have been right on target.

Thank God for the uncertainties of the first cold shot.

I loosed a single round in the direction of the storefront and then scuttled backward deeper into cover, moving on my elbows and toes, keeping the SIG up and alert for a target. None showed itself.

"Charlie!" Joe Marcus made no attempt to speak quietly now. I flinched at his voice in my earpiece. "Report! What's your status?"

"I'm being shot at, what do you think?" I responded in a savage whisper. "Not you by any chance, is it?"

"No ma'am," Marcus said more mildly. "I'm not nearly pissed enough at you for that. Not yet."

"Well I've pissed *somebody* off enough, that's for sure. Where are you?"

Did I imagine his hesitation? "I'd guess southeast of your position. I saw movement I thought was you but I guess that must be our shooter. Looters, maybe?"

"If that was the case he would have fired and run. This guy's dug in for the long haul."

"Stay put. No heroics."

I rested my forehead momentarily on my clasped hands. Moment of truth time. Did I trust Joe Marcus or did I think he was the one who'd just taken a pot-shot at me?

Ah well, only one way to find out.

"Any chance you can get yourself in a position to lay down a bit of covering fire for an exfil? By now he'll have lined himself up with the end of the service road and I'm caught like a rat in a drainpipe."

"You reckon that's where he's located?"

"Why not? It's where I'd be."

"Give me a couple of minutes. Riley's on his way in for an evac."

"Well unless he's managed to fit a GE Minigun to the Bell since he dropped us off, he better keep his distance until we're clear of groundfire. The helo makes a much more satisfying target than I do."

"Don't you worry none about Riley. Won't be his first time playing with the big boys."

"Speaking of which, how many extra magazines did you bring for that Colt?"

"A couple. You?"

"The same," I lied. Always good to keep one in reserve. "Let's hope that will be enough."

"I was trained by guys who believe you can never have a gun too big or too much ammo."

"I was trying to travel light or I would have packed my RPG."

He laughed briefly and was gone.

I lay very still with more rocks and half bricks digging into my ribs, pelvis and shins than I was happy about. A few insects buzzed around me. I was aware of the smell of something vaguely rotten permeating the air. Large areas of the city had now been four days without power. We might have pulled out the bodies but if there was any food in the vicinity then it was definitely no longer fit to eat. A tiny shimmer of movement caught my eye and I noticed a couple of suspiciously large ants tracking across the terrain just in front of me.

"Oh great. All supposing I'm not shot to death, instead I get stripped to my bones by bloody ants," I grumbled. "Just what I need."

I cricked my head over to one side and raised it just far enough to have a minimal view over the tumbled pile of broken concrete in front of me. Almost immediately I saw the muzzle flash and heard the echoing snap of a handgun report from the glassless window of a storefront on the far side of the main street.

The range was probably less than thirty metres, which was the length of a standard pistol range. If the unknown gunman put in any practice time at all, then hitting me was well within his capabilities. I ducked rapidly but the round landed close enough to blast concrete dust and grit into my face. The ants went about their business unconcerned.

I didn't return fire just for the sake of it. Let him think I needed to conserve my supply. I almost keyed the mic on my radio to report the gunman's position but decided against it. If he had any sense Marcus would contact me before he took any offensive action. It seemed like a long time since we'd spoken, even though it could only have been a minute.

Meanwhile there was no great imperative to move— providing those ants *didn't* turn out to be some man-eating species. And providing my lone gunman wasn't biding his time waiting for a bunch of his pals to show up. It wasn't unreasonable to suggest they might be looters, although in my experience they tended to cut and run when faced with discovery rather than make a stand.

I unwound the cotton scarf I wore round my neck as a dust filter and wiped my face to keep my eyes clear.

"Whatever you're going to do, Joe," I said under my breath, "do it soon."

There was always the possibility, of course, that Marcus was already doing exactly what he came here to do, which was pin me down in an exposed location and wait until I panicked or did something stupid from sheer boredom.

I could think of any number of reasons why he might have decided that another convenient 'accident' was called for. Aware my time here was short and we'd promised Mrs Hamilton answers, I knew I'd pushed harder than was prudent. I recalled again the way Joe Marcus had carefully questioned who was my contact back in New York—Sean or Parker. It was no secret that I worked for Armstrong-Meyer, but did the fact that I was reporting directly to Parker give anything away?

With his well-informed source Marcus probably knew it was Mrs Hamilton who'd come to Parker for Kyle Stephens's replacement, and it wasn't a stretch from there to assume I'd also been briefed to finish the investigation Stephens had started. Was that enough to make him concoct this makeshift plan to get rid of me?

Perhaps Hope had called him about my discovery of the gems she'd lifted from the street. Or maybe I'd overplayed my hand on the short flight over and he'd simply decided I was going to be too greedy for my own good.

On the other hand, I could be way off base and it wasn't Marcus out there at all. I took small comfort from the fact that most of the US Marines I'd encountered were proficient enough with a weapon to have slotted me at their first attempt.

Still, Marcus was no longer in the Corps. It wouldn't take long to discover if it took him a while to get his eye in.

I twisted round very carefully and checked the service road behind me. As far as I could tell it was empty. The nearest piece of available cover was probably the same distance away as the man lurking in the storefront up ahead. That meant an attack—if and when it happened—could come from either direction. A fit man could sprint the thirty metres separating us in a little over four seconds. If he started his run when I was looking the wrong way, even for a moment, that didn't leave much time to react.

I shifted my position so I could swing the SIG to cover both vectors with the least effort. I learned a long time ago that the more naturally the muzzle points at the target, the more likely you are to hit it, even with your eyes closed. And the lack of reaction from across the street proved at least that my hips were not wide enough to stick up beyond the concrete in front of me when I was on my side. So, there's always a silver lining.

The time oozed by with exaggerated slowness. I forced myself to concentrate on the noises around me, trying to pick up on anything out of place. It was difficult when everywhere was far from silent. Apart from the distant helos constantly overflying the city and the squabble of scavenger birds, the buildings themselves rasped and groaned as they continued to settle. Plastic packaging snapped in the breeze. The occasional tile slithered and skipped off the roof and smashed on the concrete below. Every time one did so I tried my best not to jerk in surprise.

Eventually, I caught the faintest scuff of movement along the main street to my left, too regular to be anything but human, moving with care. They were good, whoever they were, but not quite good enough to disguise all sound of their approach.

I held the SIG stretched out loosely in front of my body, elbow resting on the ground to take the weight of the gun.

I kept checking both ways like a kid whose parents have drummed road safety into them.

With an effort, I regulated my breathing. Slow in, pause, slow out. Nice and easy.

So when the shallowest outline of a man appeared around the brickwork at the end of the service road, I was already lined up on him.

"Like I said before, Charlie—nice reflexes," Joe Marcus said.

Thirty

THIS TIME, when Riley arrived to pick us up, Joe Marcus climbed into the rear of the Bell with me. The Aussie pilot didn't comment on the fact we both had weapons drawn. I kept one eye on the landscape below as we lifted off, as if hoping I might catch a glimpse of a fleeing figure.

Needless to say, I did not.

"OK mateys," Riley said after a few minutes in the air, "Somebody want to tell me what the bloody hell that was all about?"

Marcus tucked the Colt away under his shirt and slouched in his fold-out seat.

"One of the things I've always liked about you, Riley, is the fact you know when to follow orders without asking dumb questions."

"Great. Thanks. Put it in a letter of commendation," Riley said with dismissive irritation in his voice. "Now answer the bloody question—dumb or not."

Marcus shrugged even though Riley couldn't see it. "May have been a looter."

"You think?" Riley's words could have been my own. "Most folk aren't making it this far in. Still plenty of stuff to be grabbed from the outlying food stores and electrical wholesalers. Keep 'em quiet for another day or so yet, I reckon."

"That was no random looter," I said and Marcus's stony gaze swept briefly over me.

"You think it might have been the jewellery store robber?" Riley asked. "Come back to grab the rest while he had the chance?"

"Maybe," I said, not taking my eyes off Joe Marcus. "Or maybe the answer's a little closer to home."

That got Marcus's attention. He came upright in his seat. "Be careful what you say now, Charlie."

"Or what?" I said. "I have a convenient accident of some kind, hmm? I mysteriously fall out of a helo or get taken down by some rampaging looter. What a shame there are no rebels handy."

Riley said nothing, all his focus suddenly taken up with the business of flying the Bell, but Marcus's eyes narrowed ominously.

"And why exactly would you think something like that might happen to you?" he asked in a soft lethal tone.

"Why not?" I threw back. "Isn't that what happened to Kyle Stephens?"

Marcus sat back in his seat again and crossed his arms as if afraid of what his hands might unconsciously betray.

"Why would we have wanted Stephens dead?"

"Because he got careless," I said, echoing Riley's own explanation on the day of my arrival. "And then he got unlucky."

"Oh?"

I sighed, rubbed a hand around the back of my neck. It came away gritty like the rest of me.

"Look, let's cut to the chase shall we?" I said tiredly. "I know about Hope."

That got a reaction—from both men. I felt the slight tremor through the airframe as Riley's hands twitched at the controls. Joe Marcus's reaction was a more straightforward flare of compressed anger.

"What do you want, Charlie?"

"A good question. The truth might be a good start."

Marcus gave a snort that broke up into a mirthless smile. "And what do you intend to *do* with this 'truth' once you've gotten it?"

I shrugged. "I'll burn that bridge when I come to it."

From his face he did not find my mangled metaphor amusing.

"Hope is part of this team," he said with deliberation. "We think of her as family and we look out for each other as family."

So what did that make Kyle Stephens?

"Your apparent loyalty is admirable. Shame it doesn't extend to everyone on your team."

"Not everyone needs protecting," Marcus said. "Surely you get that we would want to look out for her?"

"Even though she's been lying to you since she joined R&R?" I asked mildly. "This can't have been a first time for her—not the way she's got her moves down—"

Marcus launched out of his seat. In the space between heartbeats he had his hand fisted in my shirt, his forearm wedged across my throat and his face thrust close to mine.

"Don't say another word about that kid," he bit out, "or you will be getting out of this aircraft before the next stop."

In reply I jerked both hands up, grabbed his ear with one and his chin with the other and started to wrench his head round. Marcus wisely dropped his chokehold before the vertebrae in his neck gave way. As he lurched back his eyes were wary and, I like to think, just a little more respectful. He made an exploratory movement of his head and winced.

Well, good.

"Looks like you're right," I said. "Not everyone does need protecting."

"Like you said, I'm loyal to my team," he said tightly. "You attack one of us, you attack all of us."

"But that proviso didn't extend to Kyle Stephens, did it?"

As soon as I spoke I knew it was the wrong thing to say. Marcus lost his defensive posture and seemed to uncoil. He sat back, his whole body relaxing.

And in that moment I knew I'd been on the cusp of an important discovery, and somehow I'd blown it.

Thirty-one

I WAS PHOTOGRAPHING TEETH when Parker Armstrong called from New York. It was early afternoon, after Riley had returned me and Joe Marcus to the army camp. Almost immediately Dr Bertrand commandeered me. Apparently my skills with a camera were not as bad as she'd feared.

Besides, I didn't think spending further time with Marcus—or seeking out Hope—was a good idea.

So I spent several hours working with a forensic odontologist from the UK, who was carefully sorting through a scattering of teeth and allocating them to individuals. He was currently gluing them onto strips of card that resembled a dental X-ray. From this, he told me, it might be possible to identify victims too badly damaged to otherwise put a name to.

"There's always DNA, but that's expensive and often there's nothing to match it to," he told me, inspecting another tooth. "Superglue and cardboard is the more cost-effective option."

I snapped each completed mouthful with the URN giving the team who'd found the victim, the area they were found in, and the unique number. Only when the body was finally identified and reconciled to their family would that number finally be put aside.

I was so absorbed in the work that the buzz of my cell-phone made me start. I checked the incoming number and gave an apologetic smile to the Brit odontologist.

"This could be important. I better take it, if that's OK?"

He waved me away cheerfully enough, his glasses perched on the end of a long nose.

"I'll shout when this one's complete," he mumbled, distracted. "Now then, upper left second bicuspid...Ah, there you are!"

I took the call, moving away into the far corner as I did so.

"Hi boss, what do you have for me?" I asked, careful not to use his name just in case.

"You first," Parker said. "How's it going out there?"

I suppressed a sigh and gave him a brief rundown of earlier events. He listened in loud silence. When I was done he expressed a desire, again, to recall me. Again I refused.

I stood with my back to the wall watching the other teams at work while I talked. The military had laid down a temporary floor that could be scrubbed clean every night but the faint tang of disinfectant overlaying old blood still lingered. It did little for my appetite.

"You have information for me?" I said at last, trying to distract him.

Parker's own sigh was clearly audible across the international phone line. He knew exactly what I was doing and was prepared to go along with it, if under protest.

"Enzo Lefévre and Gabrielle Dubois are aliases," he said flatly. "At the moment we're still trying to uncover their real names but Interpol lit up like a Christmas tree as soon as we started a search."

"What's their interest?"

"Jewel thieves. Lots of skill and finesse—no smash and grab for this pair. I'm told Lefévre means 'craftsman'. Maybe that's why he chose it. From what I could squeeze out of my Interpol liaison, they've pulled off some major heists along the French Riviera, Monaco, Madrid and that one at the Cannes Film Festival last year. This is the first time they've operated so far from Europe, though."

"So how does that square with what Santiago Rojas told us about the robbery and this supposed third man?" I said, frowning. "The one who shot Lefévre and got away. If this pair were jewel thieves, how likely is it that they just so happened to be in a jewellery store—on the very day it was supposed to have a big delivery—at the precise moment it was turned over by someone else who was totally unconnected?"

"Honest appraisal? About the same odds as getting struck twice by lightning," Parker said dryly. "It happens, but you'd have to be pretty damn unlucky."

I thought of the man in the hospital bed who'd told such a heartfelt story about the woman with the ruby engagement ring.

"I suppose they *could* have simply been taking a holiday and decided to buy a ring like normal people. Would it mean more to a pair of thieves if they paid for something rather than just stole it?"

Parker made a "maybe" noise in his throat. "Might explain why Lefévre tried to intervene and got himself shot for it."

"A sense of professional outrage you mean?" I suggested. "That somebody had the gall to attempt a half-arsed job in front of him?"

"Something like that, yeah—if that's what happened."

I considered that one for a moment. Across from me, the fingerprint expert, also from the UK, was hunched over her workstation. She had just made a match between a palm-print taken from the kitchen counter at the home of a missing person and one of our victims. There was no sense of triumph or satisfaction, though, only sorrow. It was her first time with a DVI team. I wondered if she'd stay the course or volunteer again.

"I think I need to go back and talk to Rojas again," I said to Parker. "It sounds like he may not have been entirely forthcoming."

"He may not," Parker agreed solemnly. "But from what you've said he did suffer a nasty head injury, which we should take into account. After all, we both know the kind of effects something like that can have."

"We do." I scraped a hand through my hair, unwilling to venture much further along that line of thought. Instead I asked, "Is there, um, any news on the girl?"

"I'm still waiting for the London end to get back to me," he said. "They hit a few obstructions. Washington bureaucrats could learn a lot from the British Civil Service, huh? I'll call you as soon as I have something."

"Thanks." *Let's just hope it's soon.* I paused. "I don't suppose there's been any word...?"

I didn't have to elaborate. Parker knew exactly who I was talking about. He cleared his throat and I knew immediately it wasn't going to be good news.

"We tracked Sean to Germany. A couple of days ago he flew from Frankfurt to Kuwait City."

"Kuwait?" I repeated. "What the hell is he doing there?"

"We believe he may have crossed the border into Iraq," Parker said carefully, "heading for Basra."

I opened my mouth to ask again what the hell Sean was doing but then closed it again, aware of a leaden weight settling in my chest. I had a horrible feeling I knew exactly why Sean might be going alone into bandit country and I hoped to hell I was wrong.

Thirty-two

THE NIGHT I GOT BACK from Mexico City—the night things came to a head between Sean and me—I made what I realised later was a grave error of judgement. It wasn't my first and I daresay it won't be my last either.

Not by goading Sean into responding to me physically. That had been a long time coming—in every sense. Even though he'd left the army with the mistaken belief I was instrumental in ruining his career as I'd ruined my own, he still wanted me. Throughout our brief but clandestine relationship back then, the constraints of behaving with rigid formality towards each other while we were on duty led to break-the-furniture and wake-the-neighbours kind of sex when we were finally let loose.

That night my only thought had been to let it loose again.

So I held him down on the sofa in the living room of the New York apartment and released all those months of pent-up emotion. It was almost impossible not to ravage what had once been mine to take freely. His initial freeze almost made me weep but then his lips relaxed under mine and he began to kiss me back in anger.

I counted on the fact that it's very hard for a man to be raped by a woman he honestly does not desire without some kind of chemical inducement. By the time the shower water had all-but evaporated from our naked skin Sean needed no artificial stimulation.

When I relaxed the lock on his wrist he dived both hands into my short wet hair, dragging my head back to bare my scarred throat like a goat for sacrifice. With a groan that sounded close to torture he feasted on the line of my jaw, my neck, my breasts.

And when his hands slid down over my shoulders to trace my spine and grasp my hips, I cupped his face in trembling fingers and kissed him with aching tenderness, feeling his body rise to mine in the old way, guided by instinct and muscle memory.

I forced myself not to rush even though the need was clawing through me. I knew I had to tip him over the edge of frustration until he could do nothing but give in to blind lust and take what had once been given freely too.

I couldn't contain a harsh cry as we came together. Sean's face was a whitened mask, his eyes closed.

I jammed a hand under his jaw and muttered, "Look at me, dammit. I need you to *know* it's me."

His eyes snapped open. "Christ. Jesus," he managed. "How could it be anyone else?"

When he bucked under me with a growl I almost grabbed for his throat again before I realised he wasn't trying to dislodge me, far from it. I felt the slide of muscle packed under slick skin as he powered to his feet, lifting me, taking me with him. We made it as far as the wall by the bedroom, knocking aside a small table.

My back hit the door frame and my limbs wrapped tight around him as he thrust upward with his face buried in my neck, his teeth on my skin and my name on his lips.

That alone was enough to undo me. I came apart in his arms. If the neighbours had been sleeping, I would surely have woken them.

Almost at once Sean tried to pull back. I tightened my grip.

"Charlie!" His voice was raw. "I can't hold on much longer, and I'm not using—"

"Had a coil fitted," I gasped against his ear. "Not taking chances after last time..."

If I could have taken the words back I would have done. I knew he'd registered the importance of them by the way he stiffened, then my body spasmed afresh and he was barging into the bedroom itself, tumbling onto the bed with me wedged beneath him.

I landed hard on the mattress still clenched greedily around him.

Afterwards we lay together, separated only by the width of our thoughts. We sprawled on our backs while the sweat cooled on our bodies and the only sound was the slowing beat of our hearts as we came back to ourselves.

I didn't speak. I couldn't think of anything to say that wasn't trite.

Sean shifted, his short hair rasping against the pillow as he turned towards me. I tensed involuntarily. I couldn't help it. Those dark unfathomable eyes probed mine. I knew I needed to say something but nothing came.

"I take it back," Sean said then and I couldn't get a lock on his tone. "If you'd been fucking Parker all the time you were away you wouldn't have been so..."

"Desperate?" I supplied.

He almost smiled. "I was going to say 'ardent' but I suppose boils down to the same thing."

I stared up at the high ceiling and felt my heart splintering into shards like a bullet through glass.

"I've never been unfaithful to you, Sean."

"It was mine, wasn't it—the child you lost?" And when shock kept me mute he recounted with deadly accuracy, "You said you'd had a coil fitted, because you weren't taking any chances 'after last time'. Was it...before we left the UK?"

I rolled away from him slowly onto my side and curled my knees up toward my chest, resisting the urge to cry. "Was getting myself pregnant the only reason I got to tag along with you to New York you mean?" I asked with brittle dignity. "No, it wasn't."

I heard the gush of his outward breath, felt the mattress sway as he propped himself up on one elbow. His hand smoothed across my hip and gently tugged me over onto my back again so he could see my face.

"I'm sorry, Charlie," he said then, his voice low. "I know how hard this is—for both of us. We're neither of us the people we remember."

I recognised the olive branch for what it was, but still couldn't prevent a hurt question. "Was I *ever* the kind of person who would have tried to trap you with an unwanted child?"

He rubbed his fingers across the scar at his temple and shook his head as much to clear it as in denial. "I just... don't know," he said helplessly. "It doesn't seem to matter what I *know*, I still can't shake the feeling we're bad for each other—a disaster waiting to happen."

"Maybe we are," I agreed as images of earlier times and places cartwheeled through my mind. I stared into his eyes. "But I've risked my life for you, and I'd do it again tomorrow without hesitation."

His hand dropped away from his face, a sudden intensity about him.

"Those two spent rounds you carry everywhere with you like a talisman," he said at last, frowning as if until the words were out there he hadn't known what he'd been about to say.

I nodded. "We were facing a gunman with a hostage," I said, matter-of-fact. "I was wearing body armour. You weren't. So, I...put myself between the two of you."

Sean's gaze flicked over my body as though searching for the extra scars. "Supposing he'd gone for a head shot?" he asked quietly.

"He might have done, but he didn't," I said. "I didn't think he was good enough—and he wanted to be sure. Two in the chest will usually get the job done."

His mouth twisted. "Is that something else I taught you?"

"Yes."

I could have said more—there was so much more to be said—but I lapsed into silence, for all the good it did me. Sean always had been able to read me like an open book.

"What else is there, Charlie?" And when I would have rolled away again he caught my wrist, held it fast and demanded roughly, "Tell me."

So I told him. It was only when I got that phone call from Parker I realised what a mistake it was but at the time it was a relief to finally get it out in the open.

About how being prepared to die for him was only part of the story. About how I discovered while he was in his coma that I was also prepared to kill for him. Not in the midst of a fire fight where saving one life gave you no choice but to take another. But later, with icy calculation. To stalk a target like prey.

"You told me once you thought I had all the makings of a cold-blooded killer. Someone who didn't just have the ability to aim—someone who had what it took to pull the trigger for real," I said. "Turns out you were right."

Thirty-three

ON MY FOURTH MORNING with R&R I found myself slated to work a new sector alongside Hope and Lemon again.

Hope was clearly uncomfortable about this. She was very subdued in the mess hall when I saw her first thing. Her anxiety communicated itself to Lemon, who remained glued to her side throughout breakfast. The dog even refused to be tempted by the offer of bacon strips from the squaddies manning the grill. Unsure of my welcome I didn't sit at the same table, and as soon as Hope had shovelled down her usual healthy serving she scurried away without making eye contact.

I would have gone after her then but Joe Marcus stopped me with an ominous, "Charlie—a word."

I followed him outside, noting that he pointedly turned away from the direction Hope had taken. I watched the yellow Lab trotting along at her heels, the dog's face upturned to fix her with those unwavering green eyes. I schooled my expression into one of polite enquiry.

"What can I do for you, Joe?"

He stared at me for a moment in an attempt to flatten out any sign of flippancy, then said, "Hope's acting kinda upset this morning."

"I'm not surprised," I said. "She's—"

He chopped off my words with an abrupt slice of his hand. "I don't need to know why. I just need her focused on the job. You hearing me?"

I nodded. I was hearing him all right.

"Without Hope—and Lemon—doing their jobs to the best of their abilities, everybody else on this team is just spinning their wheels. *Your* job is to let her work without distractions, not to be the cause of them." He paused. "Lives depend on it, Charlie. Got that?"

"Loud and clear," I murmured.

He gave a final sharp shake of his head as if he couldn't believe my density and spun on his heel. I watched him stride away toward the morgue where Dr Bertrand stood waiting for him. They spoke briefly and she glanced in my direction before they went inside. I don't know what they said and gathered from her bleak expression that I didn't want to know either.

I went out of my way to be pleasantly chatty with Hope on the ride over the city but she remained hunched and withdrawn, only replying to Riley's teasing banter in mono-syllables. By the time we reached our designated sector even the laidback Aussie was handing me reproachful glances.

Great. She can't keep her hands in her own pockets and suddenly it's my fault.

Riley dropped us off with the usual comms check, to which Hope responded with a morose, "OK." He lifted off again with a frown that was visible even from the ground.

"Look, are you going to lighten up, Hope?" I asked once we were alone. "Or are we all going to have a miserable day?"

She threw me a look of almost teenage disdain.

"What's the point?" she demanded. "You're going to get me sent home anyway, aren't you?"

Joe Marcus's warning at breakfast was still looming large in my mind—that he valued Hope and Lemon's contribution to the team above almost all others. How far would he go to protect the girl, and why? I remembered the way she didn't flinch that time he touched her arm and I couldn't prevent a shiver of distaste. I hoped I was way off base with my suspicion—he was old enough to be her father for heaven's sake. In terms of maturity, more like grandfather.

Is that what Kyle Stephens did—discovered Hope was the thief he was sent to root out? Is that why she reacted with such force to the mention of his name?

If Marcus attributed so much of R&R's success to Hope, it wasn't just the girl's interests he'd be looking out for. I could just imagine what the other three might do if accusations were made towards the girl.

And what might they have done once already...

"Hope—"

But she whirled away with a gesture that clearly meant 'leave me alone' and stomped off across another section of cracked paving towards what had once been an apartment block.

I knew if we didn't get things straight between us now, it would fester for days—or as long as I'd got left. Without thinking, I jogged after her and tagged her arm.

Hope gave a squeal that was more temper than anything else. I heard the scrabble of booteed feet and turned just in time to see sixty-five pounds of canine muscle pounding toward me at a flat run. Lemon's normally goofy expression had been replaced by a snarling mask.

I yelled, "GET DOWN!" at the top of my voice. Lemon was normally obedient to voice commands and however quickly she came to Hope's defence I assumed she was not a fully trained attack dog.

Her pace slackened, head ducking in confusion, but she didn't veer off. When she was three long strides away I braced myself and swung my left arm out and across my body, saw her focus on this new and tempting target.

As she gathered and leapt, jaws opening, I snatched my arm back and twisted to the side. The dog flew past me, her vest skimming my sleeve close enough to rasp as she went. I grabbed the cotton scarf from round my neck and wrapped it quickly around my left wrist and hand.

"Call her off, Hope," I warned as Lemon skated on the loose gravel in the gutter of the road and came about for another run. "I don't want to hurt her."

Hope snorted. "Yeah, right. Think you can?"

"Unless that vest she's wearing is made of Kevlar, I know I can," I said. "Don't make me prove it."

Hope hesitated. As she did so Lemon leapt for me again, although less forcefully this time. Again I whipped my arm back just as her teeth clacked shut on empty air. She was looking more puzzled than aggressive now but if I wasn't careful she was going to forget all about wanting to protect her handler and try to bite me out of sheer frustration instead.

"Hope!" I snapped.

She finally seemed to realise the danger she was putting her dog into. Seeing her waver, I started to move my right arm back as if reaching beneath the tails of my shirt.

She let out Lemon's name on a yelp and the dog went to her instantly. Hope dropped to her knees and wrapped both arms around the Lab's neck, sobbing into her fur. Lemon looked up at me over Hope's shoulder, breathless and, unless I was imagining it, ever so slightly sheepish.

I didn't attempt to go near the pair of them until the girl had quietened. Instead, I just stood far enough back that I'd have warning if she suddenly decided to send Lemon in for another go. I unwound my scarf from my hand and arranged it around my neck again. It was the one I usually wore when I was out on the bike to stop the draught whistling down the collar of my leather jacket. In the past I had vaguely thought it might do double duty as a makeshift bandage or sling if need be, but fending off attacking dogs had not been on my list of alternative uses.

"I wouldn't have hurt her unless you forced me to," I said gently. "It wasn't Lemon's fault so why should I take it out on her? She loves you enough to protect you. That's something she should be rewarded for, not punished."

That brought on a fresh paroxysm of weeping. I suppressed a sigh and waited her out. Eventually Hope's sniffs subsided. Lemon sidled out from her grasp and shook herself vigorously. Hope remained slumped on her knees. She spoke without lifting her head, her voice so low I hardly heard her.

"What do you want, Charlie?"

"Highest on the list at the moment would be not to get bitten," I said, deliberately light. "Second would probably be a bacon sandwich."

She didn't lift her head and her voice remained a subdued mumble. "But what do you want not to tell."

I sighed. "I don't *want* anything, Hope. No, that's not true. What I want is for you to stop stealing stuff from the streets. I want you to get on with your job without trying to get Lemon into trouble. I want you both to do what you're best at. You know Joe Marcus values you two above everyone else on the team. Don't let him down. And don't let yourself down either."

Thirty-four

AS IF TO PROVE Joe Marcus's faith in them, later that morning Hope and Lemon made another live find in one of the old apartment blocks.

Word spread fast.

Within twenty minutes the area was swarming with personnel. I gathered that the government had been about to declare the rescue phase of the operation officially over. Finding someone still alive at this stage was considered big news.

So, not only did Dr Bertrand arrive with Joe Marcus, flown in by Riley in the Bell, but the Scots copper Wilson also turned up with his dig team. He greeted me with a serious nod on his way to survey the lopsided building.

I stayed out of the way and kept an unobtrusive eye on Hope who stood off to one side. Lemon sat next to her, the beloved chew toy clutched in her jaws. Her gold-tipped ears flapped like pennants at each new burst of activity, as if she knew she was the cause of it all.

It was not an easy extraction—I was beginning to realise they never were. Once Lemon had indicated for them, the dig team were able to locate the survivors—a young mother and her baby—relatively quickly.

Getting them out was another thing altogether.

The pair had been in the living room of their second floor apartment when the earthquake hit. The old building, mainly timber with brick protrusions that were nowhere near up to modern codes, had folded like a house of straw. The two of them were found in the cellar, still surrounded by the remains of the sofa on which they'd been sitting.

To complicate matters, the woman had apparently broken her pelvis in the fall. By the time they'd cut a small exploratory hole through to her she was so incoherent she couldn't even tell them her name. She was convinced the hands of the rescuers reaching out to her were those of the devil himself trying to pull both her and the child down into hell.

The last thing she could be persuaded to do was hand over the baby which she cradled mute and still in her arms. Initially Wilson thought it might be either dead or a doll until he caught the faintest movement. When this was relayed back the sense of urgency kicked up another gear.

"We need to separate 'er from the child, even if that means shooting 'er with some kind of tranquiliser dart," Dr Bertrand declared brusquely. "If the child is not already near to dying, it soon will be."

I was all for it, but the suggestion did not meet with general approval. Meanwhile, Joe Marcus had assessed the state of the structure and was not encouraging.

"It we weaken one critical piece of support, the entire building could pancake on top of them," he said. "I'm amazed it's lasted this long with the aftershocks we've gotten over the last couple of days."

A plan was hastily devised to dig down outside the footprint of the building itself and go directly into the cellar by tunnelling through what remained of the foundations. It sounded like lunacy to me but everybody else nodded their heads gravely. Wilson volunteered to be first into the hole.

"I'll drag her out by force if I have to, eh?"

But by the time they'd scratched their way through concrete, hardcore, earth and stone—a job which could not be done either quickly or quietly—the woman was in the throes of a complete meltdown. When Wilson squeezed in alongside her she lashed out with fists and whatever loose objects she could find to throw.

"Crazy bitch," Wilson said, climbing stiffly out of the hole and touching his fingers to a sliced wound on his cheek. "At this rate the lassie's gonna bring the thing down on herself and the wee bairn."

"Would it help to have a female face with you?" I asked.

Joe Marcus shook his head immediately. "I'm not risking Alex getting herself injured. She needs all her fingers working just the way they are."

"Actually, I was thinking of using someone far more expendable," I said. "Me, in fact."

It was interesting to note there were far fewer objections to that idea than to suggestions the French surgeon should put herself in any danger. Always nice to know your own worth.

Wilson rooted through his pack for a plaster large enough to cover his cheek. I borrowed a harness and what looked like a cycling helmet with an LED light attached from one of the other dig team members and waited for a final decision. It didn't take long before Marcus headed over.

"OK, Charlie, you're good to go. We're running out of time so this is your last chance to back out." His tone offered no opportunity for second thoughts.

I shook my head. "No thanks," I said. "I'm all set."

Wilson grinned at me. "Ladies first then, eh?"

I clipped the polypropylene recovery line to my harness and jumped down into the hole, then switched on my head lamp and slid head first into the short tunnel through the foundations. I low-crawled on my belly, using my elbows and the toes of my boots for purchase and wishing there had been time to dig a bigger hole.

When I emerged into the tiny cavern that was the cellar, the first thing that hit me was the four-day stench, acrid enough to make me gag. The second thing was a piece of brick, which bounced off the side of my helmet, accompanied by an inarticulate scream from the trapped woman.

"Please, I'm here to help," I said loud enough to be heard above her wailing. "We just want to get you out of here."

In the beam of my light her wild eyes showed briefly from beneath a matted tangle of hair. She threw another rock but with less force, as if she'd exhausted what little energy she had left. Still clutched in her left hand was the dirty bundle of rags. I feared the worst, but as I emerged from the tunnel she squeezed the bundle tighter and it let out a feeble squawk of protest.

I kept talking, trying to reassure her, but I knew I was fighting a losing battle. And when Wilson began to shimmy out into the cellar behind me, she became almost hysterical. Given the circumstances I couldn't really blame her for that.

"What the feck do we do now?" Wilson muttered.

I rolled my eyes. If we'd been faced with a berserk man he would have had no qualms but this had him floored.

"Get ready to catch," I said, and launched myself across the gap.

I tried to go as gently on the woman as I could, which wasn't easy when she rained blows on my head and shoulders as soon as I was within range. But barely being able to move her hips put her at a disadvantage. I was able to get behind her far enough to put a solid lock onto her neck and press hard with my forearms at either side, restricting the blood flow to her brain. Already weakened, she was unconscious inside ten seconds. A startled Wilson managed to grab the baby as it slipped from her grasp. I fumbled in a pouch on my belt and secured her hands with a plastic zip-tie while I had the chance.

"You want to take the bairn out and drag the stretcher back in here?" he asked.

I eyed the filthy dripping baby he was offering toward me and hastily nodded to the mother. "What if she comes round while I'm gone?"

He grimaced. "Ah, good point. Back in a jiffy then, eh?" As he squeezed himself into the confined exit I heard a muffled, "Jesus, wee feller, you stink to high heaven."

I thought I'd got the better end of the deal, but no sooner had the Scot's feet disappeared into the tunnel than the earth around me began to shudder.

Thirty-five

AS SOON AS the aftershock hit, the building above me started to groan like an old ship. I'd never suffered from claustrophobia but that sound brought me close to panic.

Most of the time the threats I face are small. Even in Mexico City, where we came under attack from an organised fighting force, I knew it was made up of small individual units. Men, who lived and breathed and bled and died like the rest of us. An earthquake is an implacable monster bigger than a mountain. At five storeys high, the building we were in represented a fraction of it.

And suddenly I felt very small and very puny by comparison.

I swung my head so the beam of my light shone towards the tunnel entrance. No sign of Wilson.

"Come on, come. Get your bloody arse into gear." The shuddering picked up a notch. I eyed what was left of the cellar ceiling with alarm and muttered, "Not you!"

Dust speckled through the beam of the light as it fell. Over in a dark corner a skewed beam creaked and shifted and then let go with a tremendous dry crack like a rifle shot. I threw myself face down over the woman's upper body as shrapnel splinters peppered my back.

I glanced across at the hole again, willing myself not to dive for it while I still could. Beneath me, the woman stirred and moaned. I lifted away from her.

The earth gave a violent heave and I heard the slithering tumble of stones and roof tiles and crashing timbers. It was hard to tell if they were directly above or outside. But if they'd fallen into the hole at the far end of the tunnel...

The woman came round groggily. She struggled against the restraints but without any force—she was spent. Nevertheless, I daren't leave her.

This time, when I looked to the tunnel I saw the flickering of a light, the beam widening as it came nearer. A moment later Wilson's grimy face shoved through, breathing hard. The relief was like a solid mass lifted from my chest.

"Aw, you could at least have brought me back a double espresso," I drawled. "And a couple of those little caramel biscuits."

Wilson grinned wearily. "I can go back if you like?"

He slithered round and dragged the rolled-up caving stretcher into the cellar behind him. It was made of canvas reinforced by wooden slats like the battens in a sail. We unrolled it quickly and tucked it underneath the woman as carefully as we could. She still shrieked with pain at every movement. We secured her in place with the kind of wide buckled straps you'd expect to see on a straitjacket. There was already a rope attached to the foot end.

We lined the loaded stretcher up with tunnel and Wilson jerked twice on the rope. Almost immediately the slack was taken up and the stretcher began to inch forward into the void. The ground shivered and the woman screamed again, in fear this time. I couldn't say I blamed her for that.

"Do you want to go first—give her a shove?" I asked.

"Better you do it," Wilson said.

I caught something in his voice and turned so I could put him in the beam of my light. I saw way he was holding his left arm stiffly, and the blood on his sleeve.

"Glass," he said. "Bloody window dropped on me as I was handing the baby over. Lucky it didn't cut the wee feller's head off."

My eyes widened, but I simply nodded and scrambled into the tunnel. There'd be time for talk later—or not at all. I put both hands against the woman's shoulders and dug the toes of my boots in harder than was necessary. The stretcher shot out of the other end like a champagne cork and was hoisted out of the hole. As soon as I was clear I turned, grabbed Wilson's outstretched right hand and hauled him free before the pair of us were hurriedly dragged back to ground level.

I saw the reason for the haste when I turned back to look at the building we'd just been underneath. I swear the whole thing was swaying gently, as if one more good shake would see it all come crashing down.

Thirty-six

AS SOON AS RILEY HAD MOTHER and child strapped down he lifted off in the Bell, pirouetting as he rose, and headed straight for the main hospital with Dr Bertrand stabilising her patients en route.

It wasn't until I'd stripped out of my borrowed harness and helmet that I realised Hope and Lemon had gone too. I searched for Joe Marcus but realised the R&R team had all climbed aboard and left me behind.

Like I said—always nice to know your own worth.

I found Wilson sitting in the load bay of his dig team's police transport helo having his lacerated arm seen to. In daylight the wound looked far nastier than it had done underground in the dark.

"Hospital," one of the medics decided. "I hope your shots are up to date."

"If not they soon will be, eh?"

He saw me and gave a sober nod. The medic gave me a pat on the shoulder as he left. With these guys that passed for high praise.

"If you're heading that way, can I hitch a ride?"

"Don't see why not. Marcus left you behind, did he?"

I shrugged, not trusting myself to speak. Wilson's voice turned quietly serious.

"You wanna watch yourself there."

I stilled. "Meaning?"

He raised a hand in mock surrender. "Hey, don't be giving me the daggered looks. Just something I overheard, that's all."

"Wilson...Just spit it out, will you?"

"Well, when I brought out the wee bairn and the whole bloody place started shaking and that bloody window tried to guillotine me—" he lifted the shoulder of his injured arm, "—I heard Marcus say to that French doctor about how maybe this would be an ideal time to cut their losses."

"Cut their losses?"

"They were talking about leaving the pair of you down there, Charlie. Why d'you think I came back in, even bleeding like a stuck pig, eh?"

"Don't you mean 'knight in shining armour'?" I corrected.

"Forget it." He grinned again although he was clearly fast exhausting his supply. "No big thing, eh?"

"Yes it is," I said. "And I won't forget."

Wilson's stocky police pilot opened the door to the cockpit and hoisted himself in. He pulled on his headset and looked over his shoulder, making a thumbs-up or thumbs-down gesture of enquiry.

Wilson gave him a thumbs-up and eased back from the edge of the load bay. I hopped in alongside him and strapped in. The police helo had no more creature comforts than R&R's, except the seats were more firmly bolted down and had a fixture which, I assumed, was where they could secure a prisoner's handcuffs for transit.

The flight to the hospital complex didn't take long. Oh for one of these to beat traffic back home in New York.

But New York was not really my home, I realised suddenly. It was where I happened to be living. If the situation between Sean and me could not be retrieved, how much longer could I stay there?

I cursed the impulse that had made me confess my sins to him. All our troubles, it seemed, stemmed from me either saying too much or not enough. The next time I saw him I swore I would say everything I had to—everything I should have said a long time ago—even if it was the last time I got the chance.

If I ever saw him again.

I pulled out my phone intending to call Parker for a progress report on that front, but the noise inside the Eurocopter's cabin made it impractical. Reluctantly, I slid the phone back into my pocket, noting Wilson's eyes on me as I did so. I wasn't sure if the look he gave me was sympathy or cynicism.

The police obviously had priority landing rights and were able to set down closer to the main entrance in the spot usually reserved for air ambulances. As soon as we were on the ground and the engines began to spin down I patted the pilot on the shoulder by way of thanks and jumped out, snagging the first person I saw in medical garb.

Fortunately, Dr Bertrand made enough of an impression on everyone she dealt with that the doctor I collared was able to point me in the right direction. I knew I must be close when I spotted Joe Marcus leaning against a wall giving him a view of the lobby area. He was sipping a large coffee and gave me a slight nod of greeting when I walked in.

"What happened to the old infantry motto of 'leave no man behind'?" I asked.

The look he gave me was a sour one. "You expected us to wait around for you when we had casualties to transport?"

That wasn't what I'd been referring to and I was pretty sure he knew it, but arguing the point would not have got me far. I glanced about the lobby although I already knew he was alone.

"Where's Hope?"

He took another sip of coffee and swallowed before answering. "With Riley in the Bell. They don't allow rescue dogs in here."

Any question about why they'd left me behind would have sounded like a complaining child, so I restricted myself to pointing out mildly, "I can't protect her if you whisk her away from me the moment I'm not looking."

"Then maybe you should have been looking."

"Yeah, well, that's a bit difficult from a hole in the ground."

He raised an eyebrow as if I'd just answered my own question. "You're either a bodyguard or you're one of the team, Charlie. Can't be both."

"So you didn't consider Kyle Stephens one of the team either?"

Again he treated me to his best Marine Corps hard stare. It was getting harder to feign indifference to it.

"No, I believe it was Stephens who made that decision."

Before I could query that statement, the lift doors opened across the other side of the lobby and a man in a wheelchair emerged, being pushed by one of the nursing staff.

I recognised the man right away even in his street clothes. Santiago Rojas was pale and clammy under the artificial strip lights, his jacket hanging awkwardly around the cast on his arm. Half his head was still wrapped in dressings and he looked as though the short ride down from his bed had already exhausted him. Balanced on his lap was a paper bag which I assumed contained his old clothing. They'd had to cut most of it off him so there can't have been much worth keeping.

Marcus spotted Rojas too and he levered away from the wall, dropping his empty cup into a cylinder bin while he waited for the pair to reach us. I wondered briefly if anything was better than staying to answer my questions.

"Señor Rojas," he said. "You leaving already?"

Rojas managed the majority of a smile. "All I do is lie down for most of the day and there are many others who need a bed here more than I. If my house still stands I can rest there as easily."

"He is not fit to go home," the nurse said stoutly. "Please, if you are his friends, convince him to stay another few days at least. His head injury—"

"I am OK," Rojas said, reaching back to pat her hand with his uninjured one. "Please, do not worry."

The nurse's pager went off. She checked it and relinquished her hold on the wheelchair with reluctance.

"Do not worry," Rojas said again. "Go. I have called for a car. It will be here soon. And thank you."

She flashed him a smile and hurried back to the lift, her shoes squeaking on the tiled floor.

"If you're going to be at home alone you might want to consider hiring someone to look after you," I said.

He frowned. "I am sure I do not need a personal nurse."

"Not a nurse," I said. "I meant someone to ensure your safety—a bodyguard."

Thirty-seven

SANTIAGO ROJAS GLANCED QUICKLY between the two of us.

"A bodyguard?" he repeated. "But why?"

"We believe the man who robbed you may return," Marcus said after a short pause. He gave the jeweller the shortened version of our trip back to the street of boutique stores and of the unknown sniper. "It could have been a random looter, but you may not want to take chances."

Rojas nodded carefully. "I—I cannot believe all this trouble over so small a prize. If my delivery had not been delayed ..." He gave a lopsided shrug.

Behind him the lift doors binged and opened again. This time it was Dr Bertrand who strode into the lobby. Joe Marcus excused himself at once and went to meet her. I noticed they moved out of earshot before they began speaking in low tones.

"Who is the lady?" Rojas asked.

"Dr Bertrand. She's the one who treated you at the scene."

"Ahh, then I must thank her also before I leave."

"I'm sure she'll appreciate that," I said, mentally crossing my fingers.

"Did you find out any more about the beautiful young lady with the ruby ring?" he asked then. "Dubois, I think you said her name was."

I shook my head. "It turns out Gabrielle Dubois was not her real name. She and her partner, Enzo Lefévre, were jewel thieves wanted by Interpol," I said. "Looks like there may have been more than one plan in the works to rob you."

"No! I cannot believe it. They seemed so...ordinary. And so much in love. Do you know...what was her real name?"

"That we don't know—yet. We have someone working on it."

Marcus and Dr Bertrand finished their conversation and came over. To my surprise she offered the injured man a smile that was at least polite if not exactly effusive.

"*Hola Señor Rojas. ¿Cómo se siente?*" she rattled off in Spanish.

Rojas looked momentarily stunned, then he stumbled into speech. "M—*mucho mejor, gracias. Gracias a su pericia. Sin usted...*"

My own Spanish had improved working for Parker, to the point where I could work out she'd asked how he was feeling and he'd told her he was much better, thanks to her expertise, because without her...

She paused as if to consider and then nodded her agreement with his evaluation.

A harried-looking woman in a white coat appeared from a doorway and hovered where she could catch Dr Bertrand's attention.

"If you will excuse me, I 'ave a patient to attend to." To Marcus she added a curt, "I will not be long. Wait 'ere."

And then swept out without waiting for a response from either man.

Rojas subsided into his wheelchair looking a little overwhelmed by the encounter.

"She is a force of nature, is she not?"

Marcus's mouth twitched up at one corner. "That she is."

"I would very much like, if it is possible, to say thank you also to Hope and the dog who found me. Is she here?"

"They're outside," Marcus said. "You'll see R&R's helo sitting out on the parking lot. She's there with the pilot who brought you in." His eyes flicked to me. "I'm sure Charlie will be happy to take you."

"Excellent," Rojas said. "But I do not want to be any trouble?"

I wondered what Dr Bertrand intended to discuss with Joe Marcus that was so urgent, and too private to have me around. I hid my irritation behind a smile and gripped the handles of the wheelchair. "No trouble."

But almost as soon as we got outside, my cellphone rang insistently in my pocket. I halted to fish it out and check in the incoming number. Parker.

"I'm very sorry," I said to Rojas. "It's my boss and I really need to speak with him. Are you OK for a few minutes?" The wheelchair was not one the occupant could propel themselves.

"Do not worry. I think I see the helicopter Mr Marcus talked of—the parking lot is just behind those tents over there, yes? And I am sure if I become lost then I can ask the way. Please, I think I can manage to go to meet my rescuers on my feet, if you would not mind returning this?" He tapped the arms of the wheelchair.

The phone continued to ring. "Of course," I said, already stabbing my thumb on the receive button. "Thank you. If you're sure?"

He smiled. "It is no trouble," he said and hoisted himself slowly out of his seat using his unplastered arm. I watched him walk away, hesitantly at first and then with increasing confidence when he didn't end up falling flat on his face, carrying his bag of rags. Perhaps he wanted them as a memento of his close call.

"Hi boss," I said into the phone. "What's up?"

"You with someone? Can you talk?"

"I was seeing off Santiago Rojas, the guy we pulled out of the rubble of the jewellery store a few days ago. He's just discharged himself from hospital to free up a bed."

"Nice guy," Parker said. "He checks out clean, you'll be glad to know. No criminal record, no shady deals. He worked for a diamond merchant in São Paulo for years before family pressure made him leave to set up his own store over there."

I steered the wheelchair with one hand, turning it in an awkward circle and pushing it back through the glass doors into the lobby area. Joe Marcus, despite Dr Bertrand's order, was nowhere to be seen.

"Family pressure?"

"Yeah, the family are all devout Catholics. They didn't approve of his lifestyle, shall we say."

"He does seem to be a bit of a flirt."

Parker laughed. "Yeah, but you're not quite his type, Charlie."

I frowned, thinking of Rojas's manner, those sensual hands, his admission of the affair with Commander Peck's wife, and his reaction to Dr Bertrand's icy beauty.

"I don't get you."

"Well, they didn't approve of the fact he was gay, of course," he said, losing the smile in his voice now. "You mean you couldn't tell?"

"Not a flicker. Quite the opposite in fact. Are you sure he's not bisexual?"

"Not according to the information we have. Otherwise he would have given in and married one of the procession of eligible young ladies his parents kept presenting him with, just to make them happy. By all accounts he was a dutiful son."

"I don't like this," I said. "Something's not right here. Look, Parker, can I call you back—?"

"There's just one other thing before you go," he said quickly.

"Can it wait?"

"No, I don't believe it can. It's about Hope, and you need to hear it."

Thirty-eight

JOE MARCUS REAPPEARED just as I finished my call with Parker, putting away his own cellphone.

"Looks like we got that woman and her baby just out in time," he said. "I've just gotten word the whole of that apartment building collapsed about ten minutes ago."

I thought of Wilson's warning that they'd wanted to leave me in the cellar during the last aftershock and didn't respond.

To be honest, I was still reeling from the information Parker had given me.

"Joe, we need to talk."

"Oh?"

"Yes. About Hope—"

Behind us, the lift doors pinged and slid back, and Dr Bertrand came out at her usual speed. Perhaps she had been a greyhound in a previous life.

"I 'ave done what I can for them," she announced. "I must get back to work. There is much still to do."

Marcus started to fall into step with her but I moved in front of the pair of them.

"No," I said. "Nobody's going anywhere until I get some answers."

The two exchanged a glance and I didn't miss the way Marcus edged sideways a little to widen the gap between them, making two targets harder to watch.

"Is this about the Frenchman?" Dr Bertrand asked.

"What Frenchman?"

I'd opened my mouth to ask the same question only to find Marcus had beaten me to it.

Dr Bertrand looked irritated by our lack of understanding. "The man in the wheelchair of course."

"Rojas? But he's South American—from Brazil."

She shook her head, utterly devoid of doubt. "But when I spoke to 'im in Spanish and 'e answered, 'e speaks Spanish with a French accent. Couldn't you 'ear it?"

Marcus saw the wheelchair where I'd left it just inside the doors.

"Where is he?"

Where you sent him. "On his way to see Hope and Lemon."

"You left her alone with him?"

"No, I didn't," I said. "Parker called and I never got that far. If she's at the Bell, Riley will be with them."

I saw by the way Marcus's jaw tightened that he was regretting directing Rojas to Hope as I much as I was for not ignoring that phone call from Parker and accompanying Rojas all the way.

We started to run, out of the lobby of the hospital and through the maze of temporary structures and tents toward the open area where there were half a dozen helicopters from various aid agencies and rescue organisations were parked up.

I stopped, let Marcus come past me. He'd been in the helo when it landed so he surely knew where they'd left it.

But when he stopped too, staring about him, I realised we were in serious shit.

"Where are they?" Dr Bertrand demanded, catching us up without appearing significantly out of breath.

"Gone. Dammit!"

"Gone?" For the first time the doctor's voice cracked with stress. "'Ow can they 'ave gone? And where?"

"It's a helo, Alex. They could have gone just about anywhere." He pulled out his radio and tried hailing Riley. There was no response.

"Tell him you've got a pickup for him," I said. "Make it casual."

Marcus gave me a dubious look but did as ordered.

"Sorry mate, I'm a bit held up at the moment." Riley's voice over the background noise of the Bell's engines sounded as laidback as ever. Only his choice of words gave anything away. "I'll get back to you when I'm free."

"Soon as you can then," Marcus said and clicked off. "'Held up'? Oh yeah, they're being held up all right."

"By Señor Rojas? What does 'e want with them?"

I shook my head. "It's not Rojas." That got their attention, although Joe Marcus was halfway to the same conclusion anyway. "I think the man we've accepted as Santiago Rojas is actually the French jewel thief, Enzo Lefévre."

"But Commander Peck, 'e identified the body in the morgue as Lefévre." She sounded outraged at the inferred slight to her professional reputation, as if someone had deliberately set out to blot her near-perfect record.

"The guy had no face, so maybe Peck *assumed*," Marcus corrected her, "based on his proximity to the body of the woman, Dubois. Without other means of ID—like the personal items that were stolen—we had no reason to think otherwise."

"And now?"

"You said yourself that he speaks Spanish with a French accent—"

"Circumstantial," she dismissed. "'E could 'ave 'ad a French nanny as a child."

"Rojas came over from Brazil because his religious family were putting pressure on him over his homosexuality," I said. "Yet he told us he'd had an affair with Peck's wife."

Marcus nodded. "And Peck backed him up." His eyes met mine. "Now why would he do that, hmm?"

I hit redial on my phone without breaking his gaze. When the call was answered I said briefly, "Parker, how quickly can you send me over a picture of Santiago Rojas?"

There were no superfluous questions, just the sound of computer keys in the background. "OK, it's on its way to your cell. Need anything else?"

"No—thanks. I'll call you."

A few moments later my phone bleeped to signal an incoming picture message. The jpeg image unfurled down the screen with agonising slowness. When it had finished downloading I handed the phone to Marcus.

"Not the same guy," he said flatly.

Dr Bertrand said nothing, but her lips had tightened into a compressed line and her face was white.

"'Ow do we find them?"

"We call the police," I said.

Thirty-nine

WILSON ASKED NO QUESTIONS when I told him simply that someone had grabbed the R&R's helo and taken hostages. We caught up with him, newly stitched and with his left arm in a sling, already aboard the police Eurocopter on the pad near the hospital entrance, with the engines fired up.

As the three of us ducked under the main rotor and would have run toward it, Joe Marcus grabbed Dr Bertrand's arm.

"Alex, you should stay here."

"No!" she said. "She is as much my responsibility as yours, Joe."

He shrugged and let go without further argument. We reached the Eurocopter and scrambled into the rear.

The pilot finessed the Eurocopter into the air and asked, "Which way?" over his shoulder.

Wilson twisted toward us carefully from the co-pilot's seat. "Any ideas where they're headed?"

"If he's any sense then I'd guess the nearest border," Joe Marcus said.

"And if he's no sense, eh?"

"For the moment, let's just get up there and see what we can see."

The pilot shrugged and powered upwards. The Eurocopter was newer than the Bell and faster by probably forty-five knots, but unless we knew where to chase that advantage was negated.

I checked my watch. Riley could have been in the air and travelling flat out at a hundred and twenty knots for fifteen minutes now. The diameter of the search zone was increasing all the time.

"Do we know who's taken your people hostage?" Wilson asked. "And what do they want?"

Marcus explained briefly about Santiago Rojas, our theory that he was Enzo Lefévre, and about Riley's cryptic radio message.

"If this Lefévre is a pro that's good," he said. "Means he's less likely to do something stupid with them."

"We know he's killed once already," I said. That earned me a sharp glance from Dr Bertrand. "If he swapped identities, who do you think shot the real Santiago Rojas in the chest—this mysterious third man nobody can find?"

"Sounds like your pilot can take the pressure, though," Wilson said. "What's his call sign? I'll get my guy to give him a shout and pretend to be Air Traffic Control, something like that. Worth a try, eh?"

"But there isn't any ATC operating over the city, is there?" I asked.

"No." Marcus gave me a grim smile. "We'll just have to hope Lefévre doesn't know that."

Wilson spoke to the pilot. A minute or so later he handed back to us a folded aviation chart with a heading scribbled onto it, wincing as he bumped his injured arm.

"Damn, I think he was wise to us. That bearing makes no sense unless he wants to end up on top of a mountain."

"I've worked with Riley for a long time," Marcus said. "He would have given us something even if he had a gun to his head."

I peered at the chart. From the hospital which had been ringed in pencil, the heading the Aussie had given took them out of the city to the northeast, which wasn't a logical route to anywhere. I opened the chart out and scanned it. Almost at once I recognised one of the areas Hope and I had been given to search.

"What about a reciprocal?" I said. "Rojas's store is directly southwest of the heading he's given you."

"Could be," Wilson said. "Better to go somewhere than nowhere, eh?"

He showed the chart to the pilot who swung the Eurocopter onto a new heading and gunned it. If he'd had lights and sirens he would have been using those too.

"Why would 'e go back there?" Dr Bertrand asked. "'E must know we are after 'im."

"Because of the gems," I said. "If there was no third robber then he and the woman—Gabrielle Dubois—must have robbed Rojas themselves, but we know he didn't have anything on him when he was found."

"So he's gone back to look," Marcus said. "But we searched and didn't find anything."

"Yeah, but we didn't have Hope and Lemon with us."

His expression hardened. "All this for a few stones."

"Lefévre mentioned a new delivery that was supposedly delayed," I pointed out. "But he was lying about everything up to that point. Why not about the delivery as well."

"So you reckon there's a fortune in precious gems out there for the taking, eh?" Wilson said. "Not surprising he decided to risk it."

I shook my head. "I think there's more to it than that—"

At that moment the pilot leaned over his shoulder. "Coming up on the location."

"Put us down short," Marcus said. He pulled the Colt out from under his shirt and racked a round into the chamber. "I don't want the bastard to know we're here."

Forty

JOE MARCUS MIGHT HAVE BEEN ten years out of uniform, but before that he'd been twenty years in the USMC and he hadn't forgotten a trick.

The two of us picked our way across the deserted streets and the rubble, moving fast but careful, guns out in our hands. The SIG felt inadequate for the task. What I wouldn't have given for an M16 or an HK53 compact assault rifle for this kind of urban combat.

We'd had difficulty persuading Dr Bertrand and Wilson to stay with the helo. Both had wanted to come with us and Marcus had been blunt in his refusal.

"You'll slow us down."

From the way Dr Bertrand scowled at him, it was probably the first time she'd been told she wasn't fit to do something. Wilson looked pained but seemed to accept the truth of it.

"Shout if you need backup though. We can always land
the bloody helicopter on 'em, eh?" His pilot did not look
overly enthusiastic at this prospect.

We worked our way in to the opposite side of the street
to the location of Santiago Rojas's jewellery store. The only
signs of life were carrion birds and the occasional scurrying
rat.

It was strange to be in the midst of a city and have no
traffic noise. Even the immediate airspace was quiet. When
the broken canopy of a petrol station flapped in the rising
wind, it was sudden enough to make me whirl, bring the
SIG up. The canopy rattled again harmlessly and we passed
on, dust clouds eddying through the gaps and crevices.

The only place to gain a decent vantage point was the
row of buildings facing the jewellery store, none of which
were in a particularly good state.

Marcus studied the structural damage with a professional eye and eventually led us into the end unit through
a rear service door. The store was another one that had
sold designer clothing and the sight of the fallen manikins
inside the gloomy interior gave it a surreal air. There was
the relentless drip of a cracked water pipe somewhere,
too, so the ground floor was an inch or so deep in water.
I just hoped the power was definitely off as we paddled
through it.

A cast iron spiral staircase gave access to the upper
storey. The whole thing had become detached from the
building around it and now leaned at a slightly drunken
angle. It trembled beneath our feet as we climbed.

Upstairs there was a crack in the outer wall so bad I
could see daylight through it. The interior had been home
to more display racks and fitting rooms. The racks were
tumbled to the floorboards and every mirror in the place
was cracked or lying in splinters. Looked like somebody
was in for a shit-load of bad luck.

Marcus and I tiptoed our way across the glass to the empty window frames and peered out. Below us we had a good view of the street. Off to our far right the Bell was settled on the same landing site Riley had used previously.

The Aussie pilot himself was sitting on the ground, ankles and wrists secured with duct tape. His bound hands were pressing a bloody rag to the side of his head. I guessed from that he hadn't given in gracefully to being hijacked.

The man we suspected was Enzo Lefévre stood a little distance away. In his uninjured hand he was holding the huge Ruger revolver I'd last seen next to Riley's seat in the Bell. Alongside him was Hope, her skinny frame hunched as if expecting a blow. Of Lemon there was no sign.

"Too far for a clear shot," Marcus murmured, regret in his tone.

"Especially in this wind."

"Call her back to you," Lefévre was saying to Hope. He extended the arm holding the Ruger and thumbed back the hammer with a click I could imagine even if I couldn't hear it. "Call her back or you won't ever see your dog again."

"Fuck. You," Hope said clearly and raising her voice she yelled, "Lemon, STAY!"

"God *dammit*, Hope," Marcus said under his breath. "For once in your life do as you're told, girl."

"If she doesn't start playing along we're going to have to do something fast," I murmured. "If Lefévre can't get what he wants from her, she's no use to him."

"She's still a valuable hostage."

"At the moment she's just a pain in the arse. He won't let her back into the helo with the dog—asking for trouble in a confined space—and you know she won't leave Lemon behind without a fight."

Marcus flicked worried eyes to me but said nothing.

Below us the thief still had the gun aimed at Hope, although the Ruger weighed the best part of three pounds and his arm was starting to waver.

"Why are you being so stubborn about this, hmm? All I want is for this remarkable dog I've heard so much about to locate a bag for me. A small bag I had with me when I was trapped by the earthquake. Then you can go free—you have my word."

"What about Riley?"

"I need Monsieur Riley to take me out of here. After that I will release him, also."

Riley laughed and ended up coughing fit to burst a lung. "He's lying, sweetheart. Soon as he gets what he wants we're as good as dead."

Even so, we could see the indecision on the girl's face.

"Do it," Marcus willed her through his teeth. "Give him what he wants. Buy us some time, create a distraction."

"The building's not safe," Hope said at last, tears in her voice. "The gap they made between the cars to drag you out is caved in. What if there's another aftershock and the rest of it comes down on Lem?"

"The decision is up to you, of course," Lefévre said with an almost courtly bow, "but you may not like the alternative."

"What's that?"

Lefévre shifted his aim downwards and to the side, away from Hope.

"That I shoot your friend here through his left leg."

Riley grinned widely at him.

"Not a good idea, mate. Not unless you've got a couple of hundred hours' rotary wing experience under your belt. 'Cos there's no way I can balance the controls for the tail rotor on the old bus without two good feet."

Lefévre thought for a moment, then gave as much of a shrug as his injured arm would allow and shifted his aim back to Hope.

"I am nothing if not flexible in my plans. Call the dog or I will shoot *you* through your left leg, *mademoiselle*. And I can assure you that it will be very painful."

"Another bad idea, mate," Riley said, although there was an edge to his voice that hadn't been there previously. "Look at her. She wouldn't weigh a hundred pounds if you filled her pockets with rocks. That hand cannon is a three-fifty-seven Magnum. You'll blow her bloody leg off and she'll be dead before the dog finishes scratching its arse."

Lefévre let out an annoyed huff of breath and let the big revolver drop to his side. Then he transferred it into his other hand, holding it delicately as if he didn't trust his injured arm to take the weight.

"Ah well, I had hoped we could be...civilised about this," he said, and backhanded Hope across the face.

The force of the blow had the girl stumbling back. She lost her balance, falling heavily. Riley shouted and swore and struggled against his restraints. Beside me, Joe Marcus surged up. I grabbed his arm, dug fingers and thumb into the pressure points on the inside of his wrist and twisted hard.

"For God's sake stay down," I hissed. "That won't help any of us—least of all Hope."

I nearly recoiled at the way his eyes loathed me at that moment but he subsided without speaking. I relaxed my grip and he roughly shrugged my hand away.

Hope did not get up at once, just lay sprawled on the uneven ground as though stunned. She pushed herself up to a sitting position very slowly, head hanging. When she finally lifted it, there was blood staining her upper lip and her eyes were drenched.

"I assure you this gives me no pleasure," Lefévre told her, "but it causes me no anguish either. I will keep doing it until you give me what I want."

"Go ahead!" Hope threw at him, her voice breaking. "You can't do any worse than what's been done to me already."

"Jesus Christ mate, she's just a kid!" Riley yelped, still struggling without result. "Hope, do what he wants sweetheart. Please. Don't put yourself through this."

"Riley knows, doesn't he?" I said close to Marcus's ear. "He knows about Hope—that she's only sixteen."

"Of course he knows." Marcus couldn't tear his eyes away from the scene unfolding below, but there was pain etched on his face, and the kind of promise in his eyes that sees men die very unpleasant deaths. "We all know. Did you think we wouldn't?"

I glanced back outside. Hope was still on the ground, gathering herself. Lefévre had made no further moves toward her.

"Including Kyle Stephens?"

I heard his teeth grit together. "Yes."

"Then what the fuck were you thinking, letting her stay?"

"Making a mistake." And for once the contempt in his voice was not solely directed at me.

I rose to a crouch and handed the SIG across. He took it automatically before he realised what I had in mind.

"What the—?"

"He'll only take it away from me," I said, dumping my spare magazines in his hand too. "And he might decide that a forty-cal round is more survivable than three-fifty-seven. Just do me a favour—when you get the chance to shoot him, don't miss."

Forty-one

I WALKED INTO THE STREET from the far end, keeping my hands in plain view. The dust swirled around my legs as I went, like some tumbleweed-blown town in the Old West. In the back of my mind I almost heard the jingle of spurs on my heels.

Lefévre saw me coming a long way back. He yanked Hope to her feet and steadied her in front of him, checking Riley's position at his back so nobody had a clear shot behind either.

No flies on you, sunshine.

"That's close enough, if you please," he called when I was maybe fifty feet away. "What do you want?"

"To negotiate."

He smiled. "With what?"

"Word from Hope's boss."

"And where is Monsieur Marcus—lurking somewhere nearby no doubt?"

"We split up to search. He went northeast," I lied, gesturing vaguely. "Could be anywhere by now."

"Let's see the gun."

I shook my head. "I'm not carrying."

"You will not be insulted if I ask you to prove it?"

I lifted my shirt up, baring my midriff, and turned a slow circle so he could see I had nothing tucked into my belt.

"Ankle holster?"

I leaned down and pulled up the bottoms of my cargoes.

"Never liked 'em," I said. "They play hell with my back."

"Sleeves, too, if you please."

I unbuttoned my shirt cuffs and rolled up both sleeves with the exaggerated movements of a stage magician showing there were no rabbits or white doves hidden there. I even removed the cotton scarf from around my neck and twitched both sides toward him like a matador tempting a bull.

"OK—talk. What does Monsieur Marcus have to say?"

"The gist of it is, let his people go or be hunted to the ends of the earth."

He pursed his lips. "And in return for this?"

"We give you what you want."

I heard Hope gasp but didn't take my eyes off Lefévre. He grimaced.

"You cannot give me what I really want."

"You have my sympathies," I said blandly. "Just out of curiosity, what was Gabrielle Dubois's real name?"

He looked momentarily startled then shook his head. "Better for both of us if you never find out."

"Did you really buy that ruby for her, or simply take it after Rojas was dead?"

And did she find it appropriate to be given a blood-red stone?

That brought a twisted smile to his lips. "Once a thief, always a thief," he said. "But our engagement was real. This was supposed to be our last job."

"For her, it was."

The smile vanished and he gave Hope a shove in the back that made her stagger. "Now, if you would be so kind—call the dog in."

Hope's eyes were pleading. "Charlie—"

"Please, Hope. Do as Joe asks."

And whatever you're planning Joe, you better do it soon...

Hope cast me a final despairing glance, circled her forefinger and thumb, stuck them between her lips and blew sharply, letting out a piercing whistle.

Almost at once there came the scrabble of booteed feet and the yellow Labrador retriever appeared over a mound of fallen bricks. She was wagging her tail and looking inordinately pleased with herself.

With another careful glance behind him, Lefévre leaned to the side and picked up a discarded paper bag. I realised it was the one he'd been carrying when he left the hospital. So he hadn't kept hold of his clothes for sentimental reasons, then. He'd kept them for scent.

That made me feel a little better, knowing that it wasn't a spur of the moment decision born of opportunity that had led him to hijack the Bell. He'd probably been planning this ever since he discovered the dog's tracking abilities.

Yeah, Fox, and who told him about that?

I pushed that insidious thought aside and tried not to look around me for any sign of Marcus's approach. Lefévre was too canny not to spot it.

Lemon trotted right up to her handler and sat down so close in front of her she could prop her muzzle on the girl's thighs. Hope cradled the dog's head with both hands and looked about to cry again.

"Good girl, Lem," she said, her voice cracking. "Who's my best girl then?"

I studied the thin frame and wondered how I'd ever believed she might be twenty. Hell, she didn't even look sixteen.

Lefévre had put the paper sack down near her and now he nudged it with a foot. He had swapped the Ruger back into his good hand, I saw, just in case Hope got any ideas.

"No more delays, *mademoiselle*. If the dog is of no use to me..." He let his voice trail away with another expressive shrug.

Hope shot him a look of pure venom and dragged the bag of clothing closer. She thrust it under Lemon's nose. The dog obligingly shoved her face inside until only her ears overlapped the top edge and made loud snuffling noises while Hope murmured words of praise to her.

"That's it, Lem. Now find it!"

Lemon almost quivered with excitement as she began to circle, moving outward until she neared the crushed cars where Wilson and his team had cut their way through during the rescue. Was it really only a couple of days ago?

Lefévre's attention was on the dog. I risked a quick glance around me. No sign of Marcus. I tried to catch Riley's eye but he seemed as anguished as Hope.

Lemon nosed around the blocked gap for a moment or so, then apparently lost interest. She feathered away further up the street, head down and tail up.

"What is she doing?" Lefévre demanded. "Call her back."

"She's doing her job," I snapped. "Let her get on with it."

Hope gave me a look of grateful surprise and when Lemon paused to check back, she called encouragement in a stronger voice than before.

Lemon disappeared from view. With her eyes fixed on that spot Hope asked in a brittle voice, "How much do you know?"

"Some. Most of it, probably. Hope's your older sister isn't she? And because she's mentally handicapped and cared for by your parents, you knew she was never going to leave home, get a job, or apply for a driving licence, or a passport, so you did it for her."

"It was my fault," Hope said. "A stupid dare when we were kids. I was only eight—didn't know any better. She always was afraid of heights. Sometimes...sometimes I think it would have been better if she'd died. Instead, Mum and Dad were left with a constant reminder of what they'd lost. Of what I'd done. I guess I don't blame them for taking it out on me."

"So you ran away."

She nodded. "Stuck it for a couple of years, but in the end you can only take the back of someone's hand so often before you've had enough." She glanced at Lefévre with hatred. He either ignored it or didn't hear. "I lived rough, learned to get by."

"Picking pockets."

"Better than the alternative. I was lucky. Met someone who taught me. Got caught a few times, taken back home, but they couldn't make me stay."

"And then you found Lemon."

For the first time she smiled. "Saw someone chuck a box in the canal. Though it might be something I could sell so I fished it out. Turned out to be pups, the sick bastard. Lem was the only survivor."

The unwanted girl and the unwanted dog. Perfect companions. Hope's face suddenly crumpled and she scrubbed away tears, meeting my eyes for the first time with a fierce promise. "If anything happens to her because of this, Charlie, I swear I'll bloody kill you..."

Forty-two

A FURTHER TEN MINUTES went past in windswept silence before Lefévre glanced again at Hope and said, "I begin to think the abilities of your dog have been somewhat overplayed."

"She's working it," Hope said, her whole body tense. "Give her time."

"Time is a luxury I do not have. Perhaps you need some encouragement to persuade her to work a little faster." Lefévre lifted the Ruger and swung it in my direction. "Your friend here, for instance, I do not need."

Hope looked at me briefly and I knew she already regretted telling me so much. She sneered. "Shoot her then. She's done nothing but poke her nose in since she got here."

For a moment I saw Lefévre's knuckles tighten around the grip of the big revolver. I braced myself automatically, waiting for the shot. If I was lucky I wouldn't know much about it.

And then, muffled by layers of stone and concrete and brick, came the distinct sound of a dog barking.

Lefévre smiled. "Saved by the dog." He lowered his arm. "Although I think it was perhaps a bluff on your part, *mademoiselle*."

I glanced at Hope's set face. *I wouldn't be so sure about that if I were you.*

Hope shrugged and ignored him, just took a few steps forward and yelled, "FETCH, Lem! Bring it, girl."

A few more agonising minutes dragged past until there was a flurry of movement from further along the row of storefronts and Lemon emerged from a tiny hole. Her golden fur was filthy with dirt and mortar dust, and there was a patch of what looked like oil staining her flank.

But clutched in that soft retriever's mouth was a grubby canvas satchel.

"Good *girl*, Lem!"

The dog brought the find straight to Hope, head high to avoid bumping it on the uneven ground, and relinquished it directly into her hands.

I heard Lefévre mutter, "My God," with wonder in his voice. "That's it. She actually found it."

And a voice behind us a voiced called out, "Did you ever have any doubts?"

We all of us turned almost as one unit. Across on the other side of the street, Commander Peck stood just far enough back to cover the group of us with a HK53 compact assault rifle. How ironic that I'd been wishing for one earlier.

Standing alongside him was the Scottish copper Wilson, and Joe Marcus. For a second I could not think of a good reason for Marcus to be there that didn't have bad connotations for all of us. Me especially.

"Thank you, Miss Tyler, for retrieving my gems."

Lefévre took a step forward but wisely did not try to bring the Ruger up to make himself more of a target.

"We had an agreement, commander, if you recall? A seventy-thirty split in my favour."

Peck gave a negligent shrug. "Circumstances have changed, my friend." He gestured around him. "More people are now involved on my behalf and, if you'll forgive me for pointing this out, fewer on yours."

I checked Marcus's face but could glean nothing from it. Did that "more people" Peck mentioned include him or not? Where was the Colt he usually carried? And my SIG?

"But, a deal is a deal, surely?" Lefévre's mouth was smiling but I was close enough to see his eyes were scared. "You brought us in—my late partner and myself—for this job because you were told you could trust us. Is it unreasonable to expect that you will keep your word?"

"Unreasonable? No. Unrealistic in the circumstances? Yes." Peck's face was stony. "It was supposed to be a simple robbery. You had no need to kill Señor Rojas. That was not part of the deal."

Lefévre took a quick step back, opening his mouth to protest, but it was too late.

Peck fired a short three-round burst from the HK. The 5.56mm NATO rounds exploded into Lefévre's upper torso, dropping him instantly. He let go of the Ruger which skittered away out of reach. I watched his chest deflate slowly as his last breath expelled and he was unable to draw another.

Riley swore again, low and vicious. Hope merely curled herself around Lemon's shivering body as the dog cowered from the gunfire.

"Thank you all for assisting me to capture a dangerous criminal, who sadly resisted arrest," Peck said calmly. "Mr Marcus, if you would be so kind as to retrieve the bag of... evidence from Miss Tyler, I believe I will now be able to close this case."

With only the briefest pause, Marcus walked across the gap separating us and grasped the satchel Lemon had brought out. As he bent over her, Hope raised a tear-streaked face to his.

"It's all right, Hope. Everything will be all right."

He walked back to Peck without hurrying. Peck held out his free hand for the satchel but Marcus made no immediate moves to hand it over.

"We agreed on a dozen stones," he said, "for letting you handle this your way."

Peck said nothing for a moment, then nodded.

I watched in disbelief as Marcus undid the straps and pulled out a black velvet pouch. He reached in without taking his eyes from Peck and came out with a handful of what might have seemed like chips of glass except for the way they sparkled as they caught the light. He let a couple drip back through his fingers, counted what remained, then put the pouch back into the satchel and handed it over without a word.

"This just gets better and better, doesn't it, Joe?" I said, my voice oozing with contempt. "Now I know why you had to get rid of Kyle Stephens."

Riley swore again, more quietly this time, and Hope's breath hitched in her throat.

Marcus gave me a long stare that went right through me as if it found no resistance. "You don't know anything for sure."

"Oh, of course not," I agreed, edged with sarcasm. "That's why you wanted to leave me in that damn cellar and hope the building would silence me so *you* didn't have to."

He frowned but before he could speak Wilson broke in.

"What about me, eh?" Marcus and Peck both turned to look at him. Their expressions were not encouraging.

"You only received your cut if you obtained the gems first. You did not," Peck told him. "That was *our* agreement."

"Wait a bloody minute there, pal. If I hadn't brought *them* here—" he gestured to Marcus and me, "—and tipped *you* off, you would never have got a hold of the stones."

"*You* brought them here?" Peck queried mildly. "I thought my pilot did that. Just as my pilot made the radio call that summoned me as soon as you were in the air."

The shock on the big Scot's face tightened into outright fury as Peck turned away, dismissing him. He launched for the police commander's back, managed to get his good arm around the man's neck before Peck brought the butt of the rifle back, jamming it into Wilson's ribcage.

I heard the air gust out of his lungs along with a grunt of pain. He tumbled backward, gasping. The effect of the blow surprised me. Either Peck was stronger than he looked or...

"Bastard!" Wilson got out between his teeth. "I put my career on the line for you. You owe me! You needn't think I'm going to keep quiet about this, pal."

Peck regarded him for a moment and then started to bring the HK up to his shoulder again.

I moved forward. Peck's aim shifted slightly.

"Enough," I said. "Killing a murderer is one thing. Killing a man because he's threatening to expose you is quite another."

And I knew when I spoke that Joe Marcus would not have missed the significance of the words, even if he did not react to them.

"What about killing a man who has tried to kill you?" Peck asked. "Who did you think was sniping at you from the end of this very street yesterday?"

I looked down at Wilson. He was clutching his side as though it would come apart without the support of his hands, and trying without success to move around the pain.

"All's fair in love and war, eh?" he said with a grimace that tried to be a smile. "Couldn't let you get to those gems first. Him—" he flicked his eyes in the direction of Joe Marcus, "—he'd already offered me a cut, but you? You would have handed 'em in, you daft bitch."

I leaned over him, several other things becoming clear now. "How are the ribs?" I asked. "I should have booted you harder when I had the chance."

"Hey!" Riley shouted, making all of us jump. He was still sitting trussed on the ground. "Hey, there's—"

"Shut up!" Peck snapped, swinging the HK in his direction.

But even as he spoke we realised what Riley had been trying to tell us as the ground began to tremble, then to shake.

"Aftershock!"

But this one was not like the others. It was as if the whole of the surrounding area was being hit by intense artillery bombardment. It jarred and shuddered violently from each impact, except there were no explosions, no heat and blast waves, no shells raining down on us. I tried to drop to my knees, to get my head covered, only to discover the ground under me had already gone.

I screamed. A pure visceral cry of terror as my body lurched, leaving my stomach behind, and then I was falling feet first into the void.

Epilogue

I WATCHED the Lockheed C-130 plunge towards the fractured runway with a feeling of relief that, this time, I was not on board. It was bad enough watching the tyres deform from the impact as they hit, seeing the puff of smoke and only afterwards hearing the chirrup, delayed by the distance between us.

"Your ride," Commander Peck said unnecessarily.

"It is," I agreed.

"It has been a pleasure to have you visit my country, Miss Fox," he said, offering his hand. "Please do not come back."

"They couldn't pay me enough," I said cheerfully.

His mouth twitched, almost a smile. "Then we are in accord."

I climbed stiffly down from the back of the police Eurocopter. A silent Wilson followed me out, leaning heavily on a pair of crutches.

"I hope this is the last time we meet," I told him. "But if you ever decide to shoot at me again, *pal*, make sure you don't miss. Because I won't."

"I was never trying to hurt you, just shake you up a bit. Thought I could put in for your spot, eh? Seemed like a cushy number."

Wilson, I'd learned, was a man who could resist anything except temptation, the lure of easy money, at which point his scruples tended to take a holiday. I wondered what kind of a soldier it had made him, and what kind of a copper he'd since turned into.

"Ribs still hurting, are they?"

"Like a bastard," he admitted, his voice rueful. "It was Peck put me up to—"

"Good," I interrupted, meaning the ribs. "I don't need to hear any more. And as long as you keep your mouth shut, nobody else does either, do they?"

I walked away from him, far enough to watch the plane taxi off the flight-line and slot into its designated space in a line of other heavy transport aircraft. The rear loading ramp was already lowering before the engines finished spooling down, forklifts and refuelling tankers converging.

As the crew emerged there were two figures among them who didn't fit the usual mould. Manners dictated that I go to meet them. Surprise kept me static.

"Charlie," Parker Armstrong greeted me without inflection as he drew closer. Those cool grey eyes skated over the cuts and grazes on my face, the way I held myself, and I knew he was assessing the damage—both what he could see and what he could not. "Glad you're OK."

"Sir," I murmured, keeping it formal because alongside him was R&R's sponsor—in effect my employer on this job—Mrs Hamilton. She looked as cool and elegant as ever, the rigours of a long-haul Hercules flight notwithstanding.

"It's a miracle they got you out alive. It must have been terrifying," she said, ignoring my proffered hand in favour of a light hug and a kiss to both cheeks. "My God, I never expected...How long were you buried?"

"Only about six hours," I said, playing it down. It had felt like six weeks. "They had to stabilise the area before they could get to us."

I did not add that the initial surveys and gathering of equipment had taken Marcus and his team over four hours, during which time neither myself nor Wilson, trapped nearby, had known if they were coming for us or not. It had been a sobering experience.

Wilson had wept and wailed and raged himself into silence—something he was not proud of now and another stick I could beat him with if I so chose. Providing he kept to his side of the bargain, I'd keep to mine.

The infinitely slow tick of those first four hours had given me time to think about where I had been with my life and where I intended to go. About right and wrong. Trust and betrayal. And justice, whatever I deemed that to be.

"Ah, looks like we have company," Mrs Hamilton said, smiling over my shoulder.

I turned and saw the khaki-coloured Bell making a fast showy landing near the hangar where Riley picked me up on my arrival, less than a week ago.

As soon as the skids were on the tarmac the doors opened. Joe Marcus helped Dr Bertrand climb down, as Hope and Lemon jumped out of the rear load bay. Riley stayed in the pilot's seat as if to be ready for a quick exit. He gave me a nod and a salute when he saw me watching, but for once he did not smile.

"The gang's all here," I murmured. Parker glanced at me sharply, but he made no comment.

The R&R team greeted Mrs Hamilton with respectful enthusiasm. Even Lemon was on her most appealing best behaviour. Hope could hardly bring herself to look at me.

"I expect you are all wondering about the reason for this impromptu inspection of the forces," Mrs Hamilton said, flicking her eyes to Parker. "I—"

"I think I can probably answer that," I said. "Mrs Hamilton did not simply employ me as a replacement security advisor for Kyle Stephens." I let my gaze wander across them. "She also employed me to find out how and why he died."

Mrs Hamilton took a breath as if to contradict me. I waited, but she said nothing, frowning.

"I'm very sorry," I told her, "but I'm afraid your trust was severely misplaced."

She flinched and I heard Hope take in an audible breath that hitched at the end of it.

"Misplaced how?" Parker asked.

"Kyle Stephens, for all his record in the Rangers, was not a man to be trusted," I said. "He stole from the dead and sold off what he couldn't trade or barter."

"So his death?" Mrs Hamilton queried. "It wasn't...?"

"Deliberate?" I shrugged. "You'd asked him to look into the rumours, so he must have known he was on borrowed time. Maybe that led to him being...reckless, who knows?"

She nodded, the slight drop of her shoulders the only giveaway to her relief. "And that's it?" she asked. "Nothing more?"

My gaze skimmed the R&R team once again, lingering on Hope. She paled, mutely pleading.

"No," I said. "There's nothing more."

"*Thank* you," Mrs Hamilton said. "For putting my mind at rest. I mean, I *knew*, but even so..."

"You're welcome."

A man in uniform with a lot of gold braid across the breast and epaulettes arrived to claim Mrs Hamilton in some official capacity.

Parker touched my arm. "We've located Sean," he murmured, his face grave. "But it's not good news."

"Let's hear it, Parker."

"Not now. I'll brief you on the plane. Wheels up in two hours, OK?" And with that he joined his client, giving me a brief nod that was not altogether satisfied.

As soon as they'd gone more than a few yards Hope flung herself at me and squeezed me tighter than bruising and stitches were happy to allow. Lemon skipped around the pair of us, squeaking like a puppy.

"Thank you, Charlie," Joe Marcus said quietly over the top of Hope's head. "We won't forget this."

"Neither will I," I said.

Hope released me, only to have Lemon leap up and slosh a sloppy wet tongue across my face. I wiped my face on my scarf as the pair of them dashed for the Bell. I saw her standing on tiptoe by the pilot's door, talking to Riley. After a moment or so he broke out a big grin.

Marcus put his hand out and I shook it without hesitation. Dr Bertrand kissed me on both cheeks then held my upper arms and stared into my face. "What kind of macho nonsense is this?" she demanded. "That you do not want to let anyone see 'ow badly you are 'urting?"

Parker's words about Sean came back to me. *"It's not good news…"*

"Because I'm not done yet," I said, still watching the girl and the dog. I turned back to face them.

"I know you killed Kyle Stephens. By accident or design. Please tell me it wasn't over a few stolen gems."

"I know Hope told you she was the one who started this but that's not entirely true," Marcus said. "There's always a heap of valuable items just lying around after an event like this, like those jewels from Rojas's store."

"And if you didn't pick them up, somebody else would, is that it?"

"We donate them to a good cause."

"R&R, you mean?" I said, thinking of those dozen stones I'd seen change hands.

"No." Marcus's face ticked. "They don't line our own pockets. Those stones from Peck went straight to the local relief fund."

"Ah...but Stephens was not so altruistic and he wanted his cut," I surmised. "Was that the price of his silence?"

Marcus nodded. "But it wasn't why he had to die."

"'E found out about 'Ope—'er real identity. The bastard was blackmailing 'er into 'aving sex with 'im." Dr Bertrand said in a cool and deadly voice. The only clue to her inner rage was that her accent seemed more pronounced than usual. "It was rape, plain and simple. If 'e 'ad not taken the easy way out, I would 'ave killed 'im myself."

"Alex wanted to surgically castrate him without an anaesthetic," Marcus said. "I offered him a chance for redemption. He took it."

I thought of Hope, of the way she cringed when anyone other than Marcus touched her. He'd been more generous than I would have been, I decided, given similar circumstances. "I guess we're all of us looking for redemption one way or another."

"That we are," Marcus said.

And I realised that I hadn't given Sean a chance to redeem himself. Instead, I'd thrown it down like a challenge, not realising that's how he'd perceive it, or the lengths he might go to in order to see it through.

Whatever he did next—whatever he'd already done—was on my head. I shivered in the clarity.

Sometimes it takes the darkness before we can see the light

Are you tapping your foot impatiently waiting for the next "Charlie Fox" novel? Why not meet a new kick-ass heroine by the same author in the meantime? Read the first chapter of
The Blood Whisperer,
a stand-alone thriller
by Zoë Sharp

Chapter One

TYRONE WASN'T FAZED BY DEATH. But as he shouldered open the door the only thing on his mind was getting the job done and getting out of there fast.

It wasn't as though he couldn't hack it—he could wade through gore as well as anybody. It was just something about this job was freaking him out.

He bent to put down the plastic gallon-drum of chemical enzyme cleaner onto the bathroom floor. As he did so he felt the back seams of his disposable Tyvek oversuit start to rip like they always did.

They were supposed to be one-size-fits-all but that didn't take account of the fact he was six-foot-plus and well into his sports. He'd shot up while he was still at school and now at nineteen he'd finally grown into his shoulders. It looked good but didn't help him find an oversuit that fit.

Still, at least they didn't have to wear masks for this one.

Tyrone inhaled cautiously just to be sure. The only smell was a kind of sticky sweetness with only a hint of sour at the back of it, like emptying the kitchen bin in the flat for his mum only just before what was in it went bad.

That was the upside of gunshot suicides. They made so much noise they were found quick and there wasn't time for decomp to set in. The quiet ones—where nana died in her bed and was left to seep into the mattress for weeks before her loving family even *began* to wonder—now they *were* bad news.

He straightened and took in the bathroom.

Man, this place is huge.

He glanced to where Kelly Jacks stood across the other side of the room. She was far enough away that if he stretched out his arms all the way he still wouldn't be able to touch her.

Kelly's suit didn't fit any better than his. She always had to roll up the cuffs and the ends of the legs and the crinkly material ballooned round her narrow waist. On just about anyone else it would have looked like some kind of clown. Funny thing was, he thought Kelly looked great whatever she wore.

Tyrone opened his mouth ready to make a snappy remark, a joke. But something about the way she stood there, staring at the place where it all went down, had the words dying on him.

"I know that look. What's up Kel?"

He moved across, careful not to slip on the Italian tile. The boss made them wear plastic booties for work. Tyrone thought it made him look a right prat but he'd soon found that trying to scrub God-knows-what out of the treads of his boots at the end of the day was far worse.

Small hard lumps crunched under his feet. He didn't have to look to know they were fragments of bone and teeth. When he'd first started this job he'd been surprised at the distance stuff travelled from this kind of head wound.

Man, how those suckers could bounce on a hard surface like this.

But at least the tile meant not too much was wedged into the walls. Brain sludge set like cement and scraping it off fancy wallpaper was a right pain.

Kelly raised her head but she didn't really see him. A frown carved twin dents between her eyebrows.

She only just came up to Tyrone's chin and he'd felt like a big brother since they'd been teamed up, even though at forty she was old enough to be his mum. *Hell, the way some of the girls round home get themselves knocked up soon as they hit puberty, she could have been a grandma by now.*

Not that you'd know how old Kelly was, not really, with that short choppy haircut, clear skin and the little diamond stud through the left-hand side of her nose. Amazing she looked so fit what with all she'd been through.

"What's up?" he asked again.

Kelly shook her head, murmured, "There's something not right here."

Tyrone peered over her shoulder down into the blood-swilled bathtub with the exploded hole in the tiles at one end and the cast-off spray across the snazzy window blinds. There was something so *careful* about it made him shiver.

"Well she puts on her best gear, climbs into the empty bath with one of her old man's rifles and blows her brains out, yeah?" he said trying to nudge Kelly out of introspection. "'Course there's something 'not right' about that."

Kelly shook her head and for once didn't lighten up. Every now and again she could be like that—all quiet. Like she folded in on herself.

It bothered him at first. He'd worried it might be something he'd done or said, but in the end he'd accepted that prison made people go that way. He'd seen enough of it to know.

Tyrone wasn't sure what Kelly had been inside for and it wasn't something he would ask. But she knew stuff about the scenes they were sent to that she shouldn't—couldn't—know unless she'd worked right there up alongside death all close and personal.

Tyrone didn't think he had an overactive imagination but sometimes Kelly freaked him out just a little too.

"It's the blood," she said now, almost to herself. "There's something not right with the position of the blood."

Tyrone bit back the comment about how maybe that was because blood was supposed to be worn on the insides of a body. Besides, he always tried to look beyond the mess to what was underneath it. Their job was to put things back the way they were before—to wipe out not just the mess but the memory.

He and Kelly had done jobs where they'd had to rip out skirting boards because of what had leaked behind them, scrub textured ceilings, take down light fittings. And they bantered while they worked. It was the only way to deal. But this was the first time he'd heard her so unsure about anything.

It worried him.

He looked at the bath trying to see it through those cool brandy coloured eyes. Like the bathroom the tub itself was huge—big enough for a family to stretch out in easily—with fancy whirlpool fittings and real gold taps. The tub was sunk into a raised platform by the pair of tall plain glass windows where you could just lie back and enjoy the view. No need for coy frosting when the nearest neighbour was a mile away.

So much luxury and yet this Veronica Lytton chick had still wanted to end it all in a way that was all drama and real messy, he thought. A way guaranteed to cause maximum grief to her family.

Man, that was cold.

Tyrone shook his head. This woman had the kind of up-there lifestyle he knew a black kid from Tower Hamlets was never going to live this side of legal. Maybe that's what was making him so uneasy—the feeling that the likes of him didn't ought to be here.

The bathroom in the housing association flat he shared with his mum and younger brother and sister was about the same size as the walk-in shower in this place. At home the pedestal sink overhung the loo cistern on one side and the half-length bath on the other. Getting fixed to go out in the mornings was a battle of wits and wills and elbows between the four of them. He couldn't imagine what it must be like to have so much *space*, all to yourself.

Bloody miserable, if Mrs Lytton was anything to go by.

"Look, if Plod wasn't satisfied it was suicide they would never have let this Lytton guy call us in, yeah?" he tried, aware that time was getting on and they were not.

"Hmm," Kelly said, distracted. "Still, I'm going to give the boss a call—maybe even send him the 'before' pix and see what he makes of them."

She stepped back, stripping off the blue nitrile gloves and making for the door with that loose-limbed yet compact stride. The one he always thought made her seem like a long distance runner.

"Kel—" Tyrone protested. She stopped, glanced over her shoulder as she pulled off her booties. Tyrone spread his hands helplessly. "I don't get it. We done gunshot suicides before. What's so different about this one?"

"I'll be back in a couple of minutes," she said, flashing a rare smile. "Until then...see if you can work it out."

ACKNOWLEDGEMENTS

Rhian Davies
Ninjitsu expert, KD Kinchen
Jane Hudson
LA Larkin
Home Office Pathologist, Bill Lawler, head of the
    Disaster Victim Identification (DVI) team that
    traveled to New Zealand in 2011
Dr Caroline Moir
Retired pilot, Andrew Neal
Andrew Peters
Maggie Topkis
Tim Winfield